H. Lloyd Weston

Road Through a Forest Abstraction X, Oil on Canvas, 60 x 72

THE NATIONAL ARTS CLUB

Gramercy Park New York

H. Lloyd Weston was born in Kingston, Jamaica. He is a multi-talented Expressionist Artist, an author of short stories and a poet. He was educated at St. Gorges Extension College and Grantham College, Kingston, Jamaica. He is a graduate of Fairleigh Dickinson University, USA, where he graduated with a B. A. Degree in Creative Writing and Fine Arts. After graduation, Weston embarked upon independent art studies in London, Paris, Rome and the Art Students League, New York. His artworks have been exhibited in many important venues worldwide, including The United Nations, New York and the Museum of Modern Art of Latin America, Washington, D. C. In 1989 he presented a commissioned painting to Her Majesty, Queen Elizabeth, the Queen Mother in a ceremony at Grosvenor House, London, U.K. His artworks have been featured in many international magazines and newspapers and reside in important international collections.

While a student at Fairleigh Dickinson University, H. Lloyd Weston's writing talent was discovered by Harvard educated professor, Dr. Charles Angoff, Professor Emeritus of the English Department and Creative Writing. Dr. Angoff who previously worked with H. L. Menken at the Mercury Magazine, became Weston's mentor and offered him a scholarship to the Poetry Society of America's Poetry Workshop at Gramercy Park New York City. During his undergraduate years, Weston was selected President of the Becton Society, The English Club. He was also made the editor in chief of Prelude, the student literary magazine where his first short stories were published. He is the author of a Gold Seal book of poetry, The Many Silences of Love which was reviewed by the U. S. Review of Books and the Gleaner of Jamaica. H. Lloyd Weston is a member of the Academy of American Poets.

This book is dedicated to the memory of my beloved parents: Mr. and Mrs. Robert Scarlett Weston.

For: dearest Olga!
Love & best wishes!,
H. Lloyd Weston
2/29/24

H. Lloyd Weston

Climbing the Stairs of the City & Other Short Stories

Austin Macauley Publishers™
London • Cambridge • New York • Sharjah

This is a work of fiction. Names, characters, businesses, places, events, locales, and incidents are either the products of the author's imagination or used in a fictitious manner. Any resemblance to actual persons, living or dead, or actual events is purely coincidental.

Ordering Information
Quantity sales: Special discounts are available on quantity purchases by corporations, associations, and others. For details, contact the publisher at the address below.

Publisher's Cataloging-in-Publication data
Weston, H. Lloyd
Climbing the Stairs of the City & Other Short Stories

ISBN 9798886932843 (Paperback)
ISBN 9798886932850 (ePub e-book)

Library of Congress Control Number: 2023918114

www.austinmacauley.com/us

First Published 2024
Austin Macauley Publishers LLC
40 Wall Street, 33rd Floor, Suite 3302
New York, NY 10005
USA

mail-usa@austinmacauley.com
+1 (646) 5125767

I would like to thank the following people for their invaluable input and contribution, without which this book would never have reached publication. I am indebted to my dear friend and colleague, Ronald A. Sablosky, whose invaluable help will always be appreciated. I would like to thank my sisters, Audrey Anderson, Judith Weston-Lyons and Dr. Zelma A. Henriques. I am grateful for your love and support. I acknowledge my dear cousin, Olga B. Weston, and my brother, Lawrence Weston. Thanks for your targeted critique. My gratitude is eternal.

A Curve in the Road

Part I

Sometimes, whether we like it or not, life will conspire to throw us a curve, in essence, any unavoidable situation of a negative nature that has the ability to impact our lives in a real and adverse manner. This seems to be the common lot of all humans, a fact that would appear to happen more frequently than one would suspect. We can therefore deduce that no one who ventures down the highway of life should be considered immune from the vagaries of its vicissitudes. The ratio of probabilities would not preclude the avoidance of such hard-nosed facts. As a result, it could be said that we are all at the mercy of the forces, each and every one of us vulnerable to encountering, sooner or later, the proverbial, curve in the road. This could take the form of the break-up of one's marriage, the loss of a loved one, the loss of one's sense of security in life, or any other negative situation over which it would appear we have no control. So as they journeyed down that highway it seemed only possible to say that Herbert and Lela Hedram, the main characters in our story, would eventually encounter a curve in the road. However, as of now, their uneventful lives would flow as smoothly as the nearby Yallahs River, winding its way in liquid freedom throughout the village of Hagley Gap – the parish of St. Thomas, Jamaica, where they both were born.

They were childhood sweethearts who were married at the local village church over twenty years ago. After the marriage, they lived a life of connubial bliss on a sprawling farm in the country situated on hundreds of acres of lush virgin land. Herbert had inherited the holdings after his father passed away. Lela also inherited from her parents making them doubly secure. A daughter was born shortly after the marriage, friends and relatives in the local community celebrated the joyous event. Nothing of a disquieting nature appeared anywhere near the horizon-nothing that would upset their blissful existence, at least, not as yet.

Herbert was a man whose chief occupation in life, apart from his devotion to his wife was the unending task of running his farm. He considered it his sacred duty without which he may as well not exist. He was a tall, strapping man with dark brown eyes that peered from behind bushy brows, much like the unruly hair extending from the extremities of freshly-picked corns, and the tufts of hair protruding from his flared nostrils stuck out annoyingly like little cat whiskers. He relished life on the farm and considered himself a bone-fide country farmer. His love for the land was as strong as the roots of the cedar trees that rose above the surface and clung to the moist earth of the smooth, green country side. It could be said, he was a son of the soil-a man whose hands bore testimony to the scars of such an existence.

Lela Hedram, Herbert's wife, was a short, thin woman with light brown eyes and a bashful smile. Because of a wide gap in her upper front teeth, she opted for covering her mouth with her right hand whenever she smiled. The couple enjoyed a good life on the farm, although Lela occasionally suffered from bouts of an asthmatic condition, a situation that was quickly brought under control by the proper use of medication. However, the stress of dealing with this chronic condition caused the distressed woman to question the strength of her Christian Faith. "Why should this be happening to me?" The poor pale Lela questioned her predicament. "What did I ever do to deserve this affliction?" "I have been a faithful wife to my husband and a good mother to my daughter. Why should a woman like me have to suffer like that?" The distraught woman tried to sustain her despair with regular intervals of prayers at the local village church where she and Herbert were married by the Reverend Swaby, some twenty years ago. Her asthmatic condition did not bother her much then.

By contrast, her teenage daughter, Ellie, was the epitome of good health. She was a girl as robust as the water melons that grew on their farm-green on the outside-a delicate shade of pink on the interior. Ellie was a good student, one of the brightest in her class at the local village school. Her father's wish was that one day she would graduate and then help him with the business aspect of running the farm. Ellie, however, entertained no such notions, after having decided against her father's expectation. Her ambition was to graduate from high school, find a job in the city and then move away from the farm. She wanted nothing to do with the country or the boredom of life on a farm. She detested the pitch-black nights haunted by the ghostly lanterns of flickering fire flies and she hated the farm chores that interfered with her studies and the normal flow of her life. She longed to escape from what she termed, “acres of interminable green boredom.”

Ellie tried, but could not escape the compulsory task of helping with the chores on the farm. Her father would not allow it. She yearned for the bright lights of the city after a trip she had taken with her parents to visit her father’s brother, Billy and his wife, Clara who had deserted the farm years ago in order to establish themselves in the ceaseless activities of city life. Ellie was smitten by the contrast and the novelty of it all-the nicely dressed people, the wide boulevards with sleek city busses streaming by, the movie theatres, the carnivals and the fairs. It seemed she could not get the blood of its excitement out of her veins. She had hoped that her father would one day take her back for encore visit, but Herbert entertained no such possibilities after an incident in which he was roughed up and robbed by a group of city thugs while on a trip to buy a tractor for his farm. He had vowed never again to set foot in the city. He was a man who was satisfied with his life in the country-the slower pace of existence, the friendliness of the people, the fresh country air and the simple joys of the local country fairs. This was the balm that soothed his soul, his respite from the madness of the world at large.

Part II

The boisterous crowing of the cocky red rooster (Herbert's dependable alarm clock,) signaled that another day on the farm was about to begin. Herbert quickly jumped out of bed. He threw on his blue overalls and immediately erupted into a loud, guttural yawn. The disconcerting noise that erupted from his throat instantly awoke his wife from her deep morning sleep. Lela suddenly roused herself up in the bed and with a solid look of vexation in her eyes, accosted her inconsiderate husband. "Herbert!" She yelled at him. "Why must you make such a loud, ungodly noise so early in the morning? Don't you know a sick woman needs her rest? I don't know which is worse, you or that damned rooster crowing his head off at all hours of the day." She shifted her position in the bed and then went back to sleep. Herbert quietly left the room and headed downstairs to the kitchen where he made breakfast for himself. After breakfast, he sat at the kitchen table and compiled a list of chores that had to be done that day, the most important being the task of breaking in the new farm boy, one Ashton Brown, a stocky teenage from a poor family in the area. Ashton was a high school drop-out who in desperation to make a living jumped at the chance to work for the farmer and his wife. In return he was rewarded with free food, free lodging, and a small weekly stipend. *Not a bad deal,* thought the struggling youngster. *That is if Mr. Hedram don't work me to death.* He had heard about the farmer's reputation as a tough task master, but came prepared to do his best.

After carefully going over the list, Herbert stepped outside into the misty blue of the cool morning air. He took a deep breath then walked over to the cottage at the back of the property where the new farm boy was fast asleep. He knocked on the door. "Ashton!" he hollered. "Are you ready my boy? It is time for us to head out to the fields." But Ashton, it seemed, was dead to the world, lost in a state of deep morning sleep after a night of carousing, and playing dominoes with his young village friends. Upon receiving no response, Herbert once again knocked on the door, this time more forcefully. "Ashton!" The exasperated farmer shouted, "If you don't get out here this instance you will be fired on the spot." "Me soon come Sah." The farm boy replied as he hurriedly put on his old clothes and then rushed outside to the spot where his boss was waiting for him. Herbert cast a jaundice look at the terrified youth. "From now on I expect you to be ready whenever I call. Is that clear?" "Yes, Mr. Hedram!" The boy replied. "Now then," Herbert continued. "Go have your breakfast which I left on the back porch to the kitchen. After that I expect you to saddle up the horses for the trip to the fields." Ashton gulped down his breakfast and then hurried outside to where the two brown horses stood idly under the shade of a star apple tree. He worked feverishly to saddle up the horses, and then rushed back to the cottage and changed into his work clothes for the fields. "Me ready Mr. Hedram." The boy called out to his boss.

The two men mounted their steeds and away they flew in one quick flash over the compacted dirt road that led to the open fields and skies. As they rode along, Ashton's teenage body rocked back and forth with the strong, rhythmic movement of his horse. Herbert on the contrary appeared lost in thought, as if thinking about the sickly wife he had just left behind. He had lately become more concerned about her asthmatic condition after her last two recent attacks, but felt if she continued taking her medication she would be just fine. He saw no reason to be unduly concerned. The horses slowed to a trot as the men approached the gate leading to the property and were immediately greeted by a cinematic view of the open fields and skies. Ashton dismounted from his horse and then stood and stared in wide-eyes amazement at the breath-taking view unfolding before his eyes. Everywhere he looked an overabundance of green vegetation rushed toward his eyes-a seemingly unending barrage of green that was only broken by a solid mass of blue, mountains-the only barrier formidable enough to interrupt the unrestricted view of his amazement. Herbert took notice of the farm boy as he stood there staring idly at the view, then angrily screamed at the youth. "You stand there staring into space like a bloody idiot! Open the gate! Don't you know we have a lot of work to do? Go take the farm tools from the shed immediately."

He ushered the youth around the property dictating to him all the chores he wanted him to do. Ashton listened attentively, and in an effort to please his boss, he immediately threw himself into the work project with an overabundance of teenage energy. He used his machete to clear a path through the thick undergrowth in order to gain greater freedom of mobility. After that, he used his pickaxe and his hoe to till the soil. He planted red peas, cocoa, yams and banana shoots. When lunch time rolled around the men roasted corn on an open fire. They caught crayfish in a nearby stream and roasted them too. They ate with their hands like men far from the confines of civilization, content to be themselves in the open freedom of the wild. They labored until the sun had started to disappear over the hills, indicating that another day in the fields was finally winding down. Ashton gathered the farm tools and put them back into the shed. Shortly thereafter, he selected a variety of farm produce for the return trip home: mangoes, bananas, star apples, sweet sops, sour sops, pineapples and water coconuts. He put them in a knapsack and attached it to the side of the horse. The two men mounted their horses and wearily headed home.

Part III

Upon returning to the farm house, Herbert opened the door and entered. Ashton followed and placed the knapsack with the produce on the kitchen table and then quickly disappeared. Lela, upon hearing her husband's voice headed downstairs to greet him. "Welcome back Hubby!" The farmer's wife said. "How was your day in the fields?" "Not bad sweetheart!" "And how is the farm boy working out?" "A bit trying, but he'll do for now." "By the way, Herbie," said the sickly-looking Lela. "There is a letter here for you from your brother Billy in the city. Want me to read it to you?" "Give me a chance to catch my breath, honey. We had a really rough day in the fields." Herbert kicked off his farm boots and then plopped himself down into the old floral sofa in the living room. He lit his pipe and took a puff. "Now read that letter, Lela." He said to his wife. "Let me hear what that rogue brother of mine in City Kingston has to say."

Lela put on her reading glasses and her best reading voice. "Dear Herbie," the letter began. "Trust you, Lela and Ellie are fine. Clara and I have been thinking about you lately, Sorry to hear about Lela's recent asthma attack. I think the drier climate in the city would be better for her than the damp, rainy climate of the country. I hope you will reconsider and come visit us soon." Herbert could not contain himself as Lela read the letter, knowing the pledge he had made, never to visit the city again. He then reflected upon the incident in which he was robbed and roughed up by the group of city thugs then burst out into a sarcastic fit of laughter at his brother's request. "Ha! Ha! Ha!" the middle-aged farmer cackled. "That brother of mine will stop at nothing in trying to convince us to come and visit him in that God-forsaken place again. Read on, Lela! Read on!" Lela cleared her throat, and then continued. "I am sure the doctors in the city would be better for Lela, than those quacks in the country. I hope you will think it over and come see us soon.

Sincerely

Brother Billy"

Herbert digested the contents of the letter, and although a bit disturbed by its tone decided to remain as resolute as ever in his decision never to visit the city again. Sure, he thought of Lela's health problems, but felt if she continued taking her medication, she would be just fine. He saw no reason to be unduly concerned. *Lela will survive* he thought! *Somehow, she will survive!* Herbert went about the business of running his farm, inspecting the holdings, keeping the books and selling the farm produce whenever he could. Although he was concerned about his dear wife's health, still he considered himself a fortunate man – a man who luckily had found his groove in life.

Part IV

One afternoon after returning from a business trip to an adjoining town, Herbert opened the front door to his farm house to find his wife Lela, lying on the living room floor – folded up like a cat, wheezing for breath. The sight of Lela lying on the living room floor sent a shock wave of horror through every portal of his soul. "Lela! O my God, Lela!" He cried out in a state of nervous agitation. He then rushed to find her medication, but his poor wife was in no condition to be administered to. Herbert then called out to his daughter whom he had left looked in her bed room upstairs, doing her homework. "Ellie, Ellie!" The farmer shouted. "What is it, Papa?" His daughter responded. "Come quickly Ellie!" Her father shouted. "Mother is down with a severe asthma attack." Ellie dropped her homework and then rushed down stairs as quickly as she could. She screamed when she saw her mother curled upon the living room floor, wheezing heavily, struggling for breath. "Mama, Mama!" The frightened girl cried out loudly. "Quick, Ellie," Her father shouted. "We have no time for that! We must get her to the hospital right away." "Where is the farm boy?" The farmer's daughter enquired. "He is off for today." Her father replied brusquely. "We'll have to do this all by ourselves."

They gathered the wheezing woman and carefully placed her in the back seat of the station wagon. Ellie jumped into the back seat with her mother who was stretched out in the car. She then placed a pillow on her lap which she used to prop up her mother's head in order to give the stricken-woman a greater sense of comfort. Herbert started the car and quickly sped away down a narrow country road, toward the direction of the Princess Margaret Hospital, located in the adjoining town. The wheels of the station wagon screeched loudly as he raced down the unpaved dirt road. The vehicle created clouds of dust that rose like little white insects before settling like talcum powder on the leaves of the nearby cane fields. Herbert, in an effort to get to the hospital on time, floored the gas pedal and then held on to the steering wheel of the vehicle as tightly as he could, almost as tightly as his wife in her desperate attempt to hold onto life. He felt a sense of relief only after passing a sign post that read, "Princess Margaret Hospital, fifteen miles ahead", he prayed they would make it there on time.

Lela's third asthma attack of the year was by far the most severe. Her eyes were red and watery and her hands were dry and creased, almost as if the circulatory blood had been drained out of them. *What if she were to die?* The fifty-year old farmer thought to himself. *Who would take care of Ellie? Who would sew her clothes?* The big, burly farmer was on the verge of breaking down. "Lela! Lela!" He called out in a final fit of desperation. "She is holding on, Papa." Ellie replied in a trembling tone of voice. But it seemed Herbert was too distracted worrying about his wife, instead of concentrating fully on the circuitous country road ahead.

The wheels of the station wagon screeched frightfully as Herbert negotiated a dangerous curve in the road. He swerved to avoid hitting a group of cattle grazing contentedly around a bend. But the erratic movement of his shoulders caused the speeding vehicle to careen dangerously out of control. Elle screamed when she saw the approach of the impending doom. "What you doing Papa?" The girl shouted loudly, but Herbert did not get a chance to reply. The station wagon shot through a barbed wire fence and rolled mercilessly out of control. It continued rolling until it finally smashed against the trunk of a huge cotton tree where it remained impaled – wedged in a tangled wreck of metal and glass. Elle's head hit the ceiling with a frightening thud as her father's body went spiralling through the air after smashing through the windshield. It then landed on the ground of the surrounding area.

The impact shattered the quietude of the peaceful countryside, sending throngs of people rushing toward the scene. The villagers ran with the urgency of the curious. Women ran with babies in their arms, some without shoes on their feet. Men darted in different directions until a huge crowd of people had converged upon the scene. The villagers stared at the wreckage in utter disbelief. "Call an ambulance!" Someone shouted. The police also arrived and took control of the scene. Shortly, thereafter, the wail of an ambulance cut through the air. "Stand back! Stand back!" A police man shouted as he tried to clear a path through the crowd for the ambulance. The ambulance attendants worked feverishly in a desperate attempt to extricate Ellie and her mother who were trapped in the back seat of the station wagon. After successfully removing them, they rushed over to Herbert, who lay on the ground, seriously injured in an unconscious state. They scooped up the severely injured family, placed them on stretchers, and then sailed them into the back of the waiting ambulance. The heart-rending sounds of the sirens blared as the ambulance sped away.

The doctors at the Princess Margaret hospital worked feverishly in a desperate attempt to save the lives of the smashed-up family. Ellie and Herbert were pronounced dead, shortly after being admitted, having succumbed to the severity of their injuries. Lela was the only one to survive. The doctors in the trauma unit of the hospital said it was nothing short of a miracle. She was treated for a broken arm and her asthmatic condition and then released from the hospital after a week of observation. News of the accident spread like wild fire throughout the village of Hagley Gap where the family was known, loved and respected. Ellie's school mates were devastated by the unexpected news of her premature demise. They lamented the fact that she was so young, so bright, so full of promise, and so full of life-a life cut short before realising its full potential.

Herbert's brother, Billy and his wife, Clara, arrived at the farm house shortly after receiving a telegram informing them of the tragedy. Luckily for Lela, they were there to offer comfort and support, as well as to help plan the funeral arrangements for the deceased. They decided to hold the service on the Sunday of the following week. Billy, Clara, the farm boy Ashton and some other distant relatives on Herbert's side of the family were among an overflowing crowd that had gathered at the local village church to mourn the untimely passing of the farmer and his daughter. The

Reverend Swaby conducted the home-going service in which Herbert and Ellie Hedram were laid to rest, side by side in the graveyard of the local village church that Sunday afternoon. Lela had to be assisted during the service after it was discerned how drained and disconsolate she had become.

Billy and Clara invited the grief-stricken woman to come back and live with them at their home in the city so she wouldn't have to waste away on the sprawling farm in the country all by herself. Lela accepted the invitation gratefully, and after a few months of living with her in-laws in the city, she started to show significant improvement in both tone and style. Billy and Clara were glad to be reunited with their sister-in-law after not seeing her for such a long period of time. They reflected upon the imponderable of life-the unknown factors that can so readily and unexpectedly interfere with the flow of its normal rhythm. Billy then thought about the unpredictable circumstances that led to the accident that claimed the lives of his brother and his niece, Herbert and Ellie Hedram. He and Clara reflected on the contradictions of life – the fact that Lela, who was sick and not expected to live, was the only one to have survived the accident that was caused by a curve in the road. They could not get over how well the asthmatic woman had adjusted to the change of a different environment – to the expectation of a healthier life, in the drier climate of the city.

A Time Remembered

(A Tribute to My Father)

Robert Scarlett Weston

Time can sometimes be as fleeting as a swift-footed cloud, fleece-filled clouds whose impermanence can often dissolve and disappear right before our eyes. This phenomenon can be verified by looking up at the sky on any given day. There, one can witness the metamorphosis first hand – the changing patterns of clouds filtering out to form new and interesting shapes that can morph as we watch the transformation or disappear completely, leaving us with nothing but memories. And what is memory? Memory is the ability to recall remnants of a particular time or a particular place, a particular smell or particular face, a particular feeling, sound, or taste. These are the variables that form the nucleus of memory-impressions that lie deep within the psyche and which we evoke whenever we have a need or a desire to reminisce.

I can remember as a very young boy, I would say about seven years old, I would often gaze up at my father and wonder if I would eventually grow up to be as tall as he. My father was a handsome, well-built, broad-shouldered man with expressive gray-blue eyes that lit up like a freshly-bought light bulb whenever he smiled. In my diminutive state, he literally towered over me, and in a manner of speaking, his imposing stature, at least from my perspective that of a skinny, little child, had the power to make him appear larger than life. His was an exemplary life! He was a true Christian gentleman, stern but loving, as loving as a disciplinarian father could be. His philosophy in dealing with his children was, "Don't spare the rod and spoil the child."

My siblings and I were all too aware of this draconian policy, and as a result, I tried to be on my best to be on good behavior at all times in order to avoid the sting of my father's wrath. The attention he dotingly showered upon me, no doubt, helped to reinforce that fatherly fact. Now that I am a grown man standing on my own without his protective presence any more, the only reference I have of our relationship is shared experiences, souvenirs of times remembered, and recollections, which like enchanted dreams vividly enhance the essence of a void.

Although, only a child, I was keenly aware of the manner in which my father's life intersected with mine and that of many others. I could vividly remember the various occasions when people would stop by our home to seek my father's help for one problem or another, financial or otherwise. My father would listen to their stories and then consult with my mother, a warm, kind-hearted woman – the compliment of his life. After conferring with each other, they would do their best to be of help, even to total strangers in need. They were that type of people.

It seemed that even at an early age, my father and I had formed a special bond, one that only grew stronger with the passage of time. He was a minister and a trumpeter with the Jamaica Military Band during the period when the island was still a British colony, with the ubiquitous colors of the Union Jack blowing in the breeze everywhere. He was a man who loved the sea. Oh, how he loved the sea! I could remember the many occasions when my father would take the entire family – my mother, my brothers, my sisters, and me for us to go swimming in the sea. Our home in Kingston was located a short distance from the wave-battered shores of the Caribbean Sea, a sight that always fascinated me. I often wondered if the blue cubes of detergent my grandmother used in her laundry to brighten her wash wasn't also used to brighten the sparkling glitter of the Caribbean Sea. Jamaica during that period of time was still an unspoiled tropical paradise, long before it became the overdeveloped, over-commercialised tourist attraction that it is today.

Most mornings before leaving for work, my father would awaken me for us to go swimming in the sea, or to take a sea bath, as it was called in those days. It was a ritual I enjoyed one which I looked forward to with great anticipation. Father and I would hurriedly gulp down breakfast before leaving the house. Mother was usually asleep, so we would tiptoe through her bedroom in order not to awaken her, though sometimes she would toss and turn as if she subconsciously knew we were leaving the house.

Once outside, we were greeted by a rush of fresh morning air and the sweet, sickly fragrance of the flowering jasmine bush. However, as soon as Dad started his old blue car, Lizzie, the sweet, sickly fragrance was quickly overpowered by the nauseating smell of gasoline. Dad revved the engine of the old blue car to make sure she was still alive. A straggly puff of blue smoke signaled a resounding yes! Lizzie would then roll down the avenue of tree-lined streets like an elegant old lady intent on showing she still had style. After a short, uneventful ride, we would arrive at the beach amidst the musical chatter of seagulls and the soothing sound of the overlapping waves. Father and I were already wearing our swim trunks. We hurriedly peeled off our outer layers and then rushed toward the beach, which was strewn with seaweed and various colored sea shells. A group of land crabs jerkily clawed their way along the beach in numbers that made it seem as if the beach belonged to them and them alone. The mysterious-looking early morning sky was still a hazy shade of bluish gray, peculiar to that particular phase of dawn.

The beach was deserted except for a few fishermen casting their nets at the surging tides, while others were preparing to set sail in their colorful canoes to garner the best of the day's early catch. It seemed that in the bliss of the moment, even time stood still! Such was the feeling of peace and happiness we experienced while staring at the sea. My feet felt weighted as we ran through the heavy wetness of the sand. We struggled and were pushed further back by the aggressive action of a stiff ocean breeze. It felt as if someone were slapping me in the face. Such was the ferocity of the wind blowing fiercely off the face of the ocean.

Once in the water, Father reached out, grabbed me, then slung me across his back. I giggled at the thought of riding piggy-back style. Then without a word of warning, and with his seven-year son pasted to his back, he suddenly plunged headlong into the sea. There wasn't a moment's time to react. I held on tightly to my father as a huge wave crashed over our heads, filling my mouth and ears with water. I gasped, feeling my chest heave back and forth as I struggled to breathe, but it seemed the awesome power of the waves had knocked the air out of my lungs. Those few moments of submersion felt like an eternity to me. The sea water rattled in my ears like the sound of drums pounding relentlessly in an echo chamber. I held on tightly to my father's back as we swam together, flesh to flesh, blood to blood, father to son. I felt like a boy on a dolphin's back, bobbing up and down with the waves that appeared to be my playmates throwing foam at me. It certainly was thrilling to experience the seesaw sensation of the waves in the restless environment of their home in the sea. I found myself lost in the joy of the moment – the wind slapping me in the face, the waves roughing me up, pushing me around in a motion-filled adventure that I would never soon forget.

Then, as if realizing he needed more freedom to go swimming by himself, Father swam back to shore with me in tow to retrieve a rubber tube he had brought along, in which he would place me to bob around safely by myself. He put me in the rubber device, after which he went off swimming freely by himself. It sure felt good to float without fear of sinking. Dad swam with the ease of a fish, like an emperor of the sea, like someone born to rule over water. He rode the waves like a water jockey, flogging the surface with each extended movement of his muscular arms and the coordinated flapping of his agile feet. He seemed to relish the thrill of every wave that rose up to greet him. I laughed in childish amusement while floating safely in my sturdy rubber craft, occasionally grabbing at strands of slimy seaweed while enjoying the novelty of such a special adventure. Father then suddenly shouted out to me, “Come on, kiddo, it’s time for you to learn how to swim.” He scooped me up in his arms, told me to extend my arms above my head while, at the same time, flapping my feet against the water. It was exciting to be tossed around by the waves while swimming safely in the harbor of my father’s arms.

I wished those magical moments would never end, but the complexion of the sky had already started to change. The mauve-blue haze of early dawn had suddenly given way to a golden burst of orange light, which lit up the sky, transforming the haze of early dawn into the magnificence of another golden tropical sunrise. Sea birds sailed excitedly above as if to announce the emergence of another beautiful day in the tropics. By then, Dad knew it was time for us to leave. A noisy group of sea bathers had started to arrive, despoiling the quietude of the early morning scene. We packed up our belongings, included some sea shells and driftwood which I had collected to take back home. We then slowly made our way back to the car.

I hated the thought of leaving but felt totally refreshed from the yet unspoiled waters of the fabled Caribbean Sea. I sneaked one last look at the waves breaking majestically against the shore in their never-ending cycle of ceaseless motion. We boarded the patiently waiting Lizzie and jauntily headed home.

This immensely enjoyable experience formed an unbreakable bond between my father and me. It was a relationship that only grew stronger with the passage of time, stronger than glue – such was the feeling of closeness I felt for my dad, especially now that he is deceased and no longer a part of the cares and worries of this world. Ours was a relationship that could never be duplicated. How could it be? Nothing could come close to or equal those sterling moments – moments which occasionally flash upon the inner sanctum of my mind, transporting me back to that day in childhood when I clung to my father's back as we swam together in filial unity, flesh to flesh, blood to blood, father to son. I often think of my dad now that he is no longer with us, but I feel very grateful for the unforgettable memories we shared at the beach that day – memories which I still reflect upon. How beautiful and unspoiled the world appeared during that tranquil period of time! It was a time when it seemed even time itself stood still, giving us a chance to build a lifetime of memories. I often reminisce about those happy moments, which are now firmly ensconced in a secret compartment of my memory bank – bringing me great joy whenever I reflect upon the adventures my father and I shared at the beach that day – that magical day, those pleasurable moments in time, that special time remembered.

Climbing the Stairs of the City

(New York City 1986)

Part I

Summer arrived in the city with its usual entourage of H's-hot, humid and hazy. The air quality over the Port Authority Bus Terminal, forty-second street at Eight Avenue, New York City, was the same today as usual – smog awful! The noxious fumes emitted by vehicular traffic in the area, combined with that of arriving and departing buses from different regions of the United States, only further served to exacerbate the air pollution problem plaguing that famed section of the city. As a matter of fact, if one were to stand long enough in the arrival zone of the terminal building, it seemed quite possible one would become discolored from the dark clouds of noxious fumes streaming from exhaust pipes. This was a daily occurrence caused by vehicular traffic descending upon New York City. It was on a day such as this that Sandra Davis wheeled into New York from Peoria, Illinois, on a gray-blue Greyhound bus late one afternoon in late July. The trip had been a long and exhausting one – a day and a half sojourn, over a thousand miles by land. She had to have a reason for such an arduous undertaking. Sandra Davis appeared tired and disheveled after stepping off the bus – barely enough energy to lug her blue Samsonite suitcase after it was pulled from the underbelly of the bus by the driver. She wiped the weariness from her eyes, as if preparing to take on the challenges of the city in which she had just arrived. Would she be brave enough to try?

The thought of being in New York for the first time filled her with an explosive feeling of excitement, the same heady sensation experienced by most first-time visitors to this incredible urban wonderland. Her head whirled like a satellite around which all her wildest fantasies revolved: sight-seeing, shopping sprees, fashion shows, discotheques, even a horse and carriage ride around Central Park. She wanted to do it all and, of course, realize her dream of becoming the successful high fashion model that she envisioned herself to be – the next big thing on the New York fashion scene – an overly ambitious "wannabe," chasing her cherished dream. She was drawn to the city by the power of that dream, one which only those who aspire to the trappings of wealth and fame could ever hope to understand. She was confident she had all the attributes needed to become the next sensation on the New York fashion scene, following in the footsteps of her idols, the fresh-faced Cheryl Tiegs or the sophisticated Lauren Hutton, both over-exposed faces in the 80s, New York fashion scene, whose photographs were plastered in the windows of coffee shops and department stores all over the city. Not even the most horrific tales of crime or the sight of homeless people sleeping on the sidewalks of New York City during that period of time could deter her from her dream – a dream as strong as her faith in America itself.

Sandra Davis felt confident she had all the attributes needed for that ephemeral but glamorous profession. She was favored with the ideal height of five feet, 10 inches tall, a factor which instantly gave her a giraffe-like advantage over the competition. She had an unusually beautiful face hoisted on top of a graceful swan-like neck – a much sort after feature in any fashion world. High cheek bones gave her face structural clarity, and her dazzling green eyes cast a hypnotic spell, one which she hoped would allow her the privilege to excel. She wore her silken, corn-colored blond hair in a breezy, casual style, which bounced with a free, rhythmic movement whenever she walked. She had full, well-formed lips, which looked almost as if they were sculpted on her face – a dominant feature in an otherwise beautiful but impersonal-looking face. She hoped her looks would propel her to the pinnacle of fame and that her face would become as readily recognizable a commodity as that of the iconic Statue of Liberty standing guard over New York City harbor. She had already envisioned herself on the covers of fashion magazines, such as Vogue and Bazaar. She felt strongly her looks would turn them on, like the light switch that threw the lights on the Christmas trees at Rockefeller Center each year. She knew establishing herself would not be easy, but she came prepared, armed with her dream, like many other aspiring models before her, some to be disillusioned by the failure of realizing that very dream. She attributed her positive outlook to inherited survival instincts. Any 18-year-old girl fleeing the dreariness of rural life on a farm in Peoria, Illinois, to seek fame and fortune in a city like New York had to have a positive outlook. New York is no place for novices. It is like the unharnessed power of a tidal wave. It will sweep away even the most resilient in its wake.

Sandra Davis struggled through the mezzanine floor of the bus terminal, her blue Samsonite suitcase pitching her from side to side as she walked. She wore a pink floral blouse and faded blue jeans, torn at the knees, keeping in sync with the fashion style of the day. She appeared dazed and confused before stepping onto the swiftly moving steps of the escalator, where she was immediately struck by the aura of a most unusual sight below: Crowds of people rushing back and forth through the lobby of the terminal building with such an accustomed rapidity of movement that from her perspective on the mezzanine floor, it seemed almost as if it were electronically controlled. She then and therefore experienced her first jolt of New York's extraordinary energy. The scene made her dizzy and reminded her of the Alfred Hitchcock movie, Vertigo. She held on tightly to the rubber railing of the escalator, as if afraid of falling into the vortex below.

As she edged her way through the lobby of the building, she suddenly thought of her boyfriend, Marc Wilson, whom she had just left behind in Peoria, Illinois. He was a man older than she, about 8 years older, to whom she meant everything. She was his pride and joy – his own magnificent discovery. Marc Wilson spent the last two months in his hometown of Peoria, Illinois, compiling the modeling portfolio which she took with her when she left for the trip to New York. He had also given her leads for modeling agencies in the city and even arranged a place for her to stay – the apartment of a family friend, one Joy Mayfield, whose residence was located in the midtown section of Manhattan's fashionable Eastside. Mark Wilson's generosity, however, was not without conditions, although he demanded nothing from her – nothing more than loyalty – nothing more than faithfulness. He was aware of New York's reputation as a place where people easily forget their loyalties and priorities after a few months of living there. "Don't forget to whom you belong, Baby," he threatened in her ears before she boarded the bus. "Make sure to buzz me as soon as you arrive."

Sandra Davis stepped off the escalator and headed straight toward the recently installed floor-to-ceiling glass paneled wall that separated the street outside from the interior of the building. She spun through the revolving glass door and onto Eight Avenue, where she instantly came face to face with one of the city's most dazzling and electrifying sights – the psychedelic repetitive movement of Time Square's garish, honky-tonk, non-stop neon lights – that same outlandish spectacle for which untold crowds of people continually came, drawn to its inner core like moths to a flame. She wheeled the suitcase onto the sidewalk of Eight Avenue and was immediately struck by a loud blast of music emanating from the chrome and blue boom box of an Afro-headed teenager heading up Eight Avenue. The music escaping from the boom box was none other than the voice of music icon Frank Sinatra, singing his famous version of the New York, New York theme song, "If I could make it there, I'll make it anywhere; it's up to you, New York, New York."

"This is W.B.L.S," the disc jockey blurted out, in a glitzy tone of voice. "And that was old, blue eyes, giving us his immortal rendition of the city that has become the Eight W-A-N-D-A-H of the W-O-R-L-D, the city that it seems has even forgotten how to sleep."

Sandra Davis rushed past the noise for fear of being deafened in its aftermath. She did not get far, however, when she was rudely accosted by a bizarrely-dressed New York street pimp, standing on the corner of Eighth Avenue and 42nd Street, ready to pounce on his next potential money-making prey – any attractive out-of-town young woman, walking by herself-someone he could easily approach and induct into the scary, New York, prostitution scene. “Hey, beautiful!” The pimp made his overture to the farm-fresh beauty. “Looking for company tonight?”

So this is New York, Sandra thought to herself. She felt a nauseating feeling from the rundown, the seediness of the Eight Avenue Strip – the hookers, the lookers, and the off-track bookers-women walking by without batting an eye, men wearing overcoats in the middle of July, sirens blasting from day into night, sex shops that hit you slam-bang in the eyes! *There must be some relief from this madness.* Sandra once again thought to herself. The scene was too much for her, so she decided to hail a cab. “Taxi! taxi!” A bright flash of yellow cut through the flow of traffic heading up Eighth Avenue. The driver ignored rules and regulations in his greed to grab a fare. “Where to, miss?” he enquired of his gorgeous passenger.

“160 East 27th Street,” Sandra replied, directing the driver to the address of the residence, which Marc Wilson had provided for her. She lit a cigarette and watched the smoke drift upward, through the taxi window, up toward the direction of the skyscrapers. Her happiness also ascended toward new heights.

Part II

In a New York minute, the taxi driver pulled up to the address Sandra had given to him. He stopped the taxi and collected his fare. Sandra exited the cab. The driver popped the trunk, retrieved her suitcase, and took it into the lobby of the building for her. Sandra searched for Joy Mayfield's name on the glass-enclosed panel of the intercom, which was placed against a marble wall in the lobby of the building. She pressed the buzzer, and Joy Mayfield answered, "Who is it?"

"Sandra Davis," she replied.

"Yes, I've been expecting you. Take the elevator to the third floor, apartment 3D." Sandra got into the elevator and pressed the button for apartment 3D. She got out on the third floor and headed toward Joy Mayfield's apartment. She pressed the buzzer. "Who is it?"

"Sandra Davis." Joy Mayfield opened the door and was immediately impressed with Sandra's weary, but exquisite-looking face.

"Welcome! I am Joy Mayfield."

"I am Sandra Davis; nice to meet you," the aspiring model replied.

"Do come in," Joy Mayfield said, greeting her guest. "Here, let me take your suitcase." Joy Mayfield rolled Sandra's Samsonite down a narrow hallway to the bedroom where her guest would be staying, then quickly returned. "You must be tired; do sit down, dear." She directed Sandra to an orange-colored wing chair, placed next to a beige sofa in the L-shaped living room. "Your friend Mark Wilson told me a lot about you. He called a few minutes ago to find out if she had arrived. He wants you to call him as soon as you settle down."

"I will," Sandra replied. "May I offer you a drink?"

"A diet coke, thankyou!"

Sandra glanced around the room as if trying to get herself acquainted with her new surroundings. Suddenly, her eyes latched onto a framed print poster of pop legend Mick Jagger of the Rolling Stones – his full lips pouting from a print poster hanging against the beige color of the living room wall. Sandra studied the poster as if thinking that she herself would also have to primp and pout her way to fame. Joy returned with the diet coke and handed it to her guest. She poured a glass of chardonnay for herself. "Mark told me a lot about you. He said you would like to be a high-fashion model. Well, to your success!"

"Thank you!" Sandra replied. "Whew!" she exclaimed "Is New York always as hot as this in the summer?" "Unfortunately, dear," Joy intoned. "You arrived in the middle of a searing heat wave." Joy walked over to the air conditioner and then cranked up the volume.

"I hate when it gets as hot as this in New York," she lamented, "but like other inconveniences, we sooner or later learn to live with them."

Joy Mayfield's apartment had an air of established neatness, a trait indicative of her well-ordered secretarial life. It seemed nothing was out of place, except the curious manner in which she stared at the beautiful young creature, who had just now flown into her nest – the gorgeous one perched on the orange-winged chair. "So you want to be a model?" Joy cast a jaundiced look at Sandra's exquisite-looking face. "Well, I must warn you about one thing, dear; this is New York, and there are many pitfalls." Sandra absorbed the remark but wondered if her host, whom she had just met, should be talking to her about pits and falls.

The older woman's concern reminded her of the controlling mother she had just left behind in Illinois.

"Yes, I know," Sandra said. "But I am a big girl now." She snapped the conversation in two as if to serve notice to her host that she would not tolerate interference in her personal life. Joy detected an edge in the farm girl's voice, but dismissed it as a bad case of fatigue due to the long, weary trip.

"Do you care for something to eat?"

"Not really!" Sandra replied. "I am just too tired and exhausted from the trip."

"Well, one last thing," Joy Mayfield interjected. "I travel a lot, so sometimes you will be here in the apartment by yourself. Please be careful!" Sandra blinked and almost fell asleep, just in time for Joy to direct her to the bedroom down the hallway where she would be sleeping.

Part III

Sandra awoke the following morning after a night of fitful sleep and zigzag dreams, possibly due to the strangeness of her new environment and the infernal noise of the all-night New York City traffic. She shook her head as if to awaken herself from a stupor, as if to accept the fact that she was no longer on a farm in Peoria, Illinois. Joy Mayfield had already left for her office downtown. Sandra made a light breakfast for herself – orange juice, coffee, and toast while keeping in mind the figure she had to maintain as she prepared to embark upon her modeling career. The anticipation sent shivers of excitement coursing through her veins. “Start spreading the news.” She found herself singing the opening lines of the famous New York, New York, theme song. She rushed to the shower as if to wash the remnants of farm life from her newly awakened self.

She emerged from the shower, a new woman in New York. Today she would start climbing the stairs of the city. She finally felt relaxed enough to call her boyfriend, Marc Wilson, but instead decided to call her mother first. Mary Louise was happy to hear from her daughter and relieved to know that she had arrived safely in New York. However, she could not wait to saturate her with an overabundance of motherly advice. “I have been worried sick since you left, Sandra. I know you consider yourself independent and all with this Women’s Liberation crap, but please remember that New York is no place for a young girl like you. I know you want to pursue your career and make a name for yourself, but New York is a scary place, especially for an attractive girl alone!”

“You worry too much, Mom,” Sandra replied. “Think of all the money I’ll be making when I become a very successful fashion model.” But Mary Louis had no time for that.

“Sandra, I was never one for you going into that profession, leaving home to go so far away. There are many attractive young women here in Peoria who swallow their pride and try to find a nine-to-five job. If your father was alive, he would have bolted the door and never would have allowed you to leave. Your younger siblings miss you and are crying for you every day!”

“Mom, you don’t understand,” Sandra screamed. “This is my dream!” But Mary Louise had heard it all before.

"You do what you want to do, Sandra. I have no control over you. Goodbye! Take care of yourself, sweetheart. Call me when you can."

Sandra proceeded to call her boyfriend next. Mark Wilson was glad to hear from her but felt displeased that she did not call the night before, as promised. However, he understood after she explained how tired she was and worn out from the trip. He wished her good luck with the contacts for the modeling agencies but had already begun to feel lost, lonely without her. As a result, he had decided to pursue his career as a fashion photographer more vigorously. He ended the conversation by pledging his eternal love for her. Sandra accepted the compliment and did the same in return.

The next call was probably the most important one she had to make. Sandra reached for her address book and dialed the telephone number for one of the modeling agencies that Mark Wilson had given to her. The phone was answered by the brusque voice of a female receptionist. "Hello, Instant Success Modeling Agency, how may I help you?"

"Yes! This is Sandra Davis from Peoria, Illinois. May I speak to Ms. Merle Mitchell, Please?" the operator's brusque voice instantaneously froze the line. "Sandra who? from what? I am sorry. Ms. Mitchell is not available now. May I take a message?"

Yes! I was recommended to her by a friend of mine back home in Illi…The operator did not give Sandra a chance to continue. "The best I can do is to give you an appointment. Next Wednesday, 1 pm fine! See you! Bye!"

Sandra was displeased that she was not able to speak directly to Ms. Merle Mitchell, but felt ecstatic that she had scored an appointment with the agency. She decided to take the day off to go sight-seeing around the city. She got dressed and left the apartment in a hurry, anxious to get acquainted with the sights and sounds of New York City. She wandered broad avenues and narrow streets, small boutiques and large department stores – Macy's, Lord and Taylor, Saks Fifth Avenue, and Bloomingdales. It seemed she could not get her fill. How happy she felt as she joined the throngs of people filling the streets of New York City that day! It made her feel excited and alive. The following day, she visited the Empire State Building, an attraction which she could only dream about as a child. How insignificant she felt as she gazed up at the towering mass of sky scrapers – monolithic blocks of steel and glass – rising out of the humble earth below, blocking out huge portions of space and light. She hopped onto one of the sleek new city buses streaming by and watched in amazement as the city whizzed past her in dizzying spurts of joyous emotions. The magic of the city seeped under her skin like a healthy dose of much-needed excitement. *This is it!* The newly arrived resident of the city thought to herself as she revelled in the excitement of living her dreams. She instantly embraced New York and felt the distance between herself and the familiarity of her past life on the farms of Peoria, Illinois, which now continued to wane from her memory. Later that evening, she called her boyfriend, Marc Wilson, to tell him about all the exciting things she saw and did that day. Marc Wilson, however, could not wait to tell her how much he missed her, how much he loved her – how much he cared for her, and how much he longed for her. Sandra Davis echoed similar sentiments but wasted no time as she continued to climb the stairs of the city.

Part IV

The appointment at the Instant Success Modeling Agency rolled around much faster than Sandra had anticipated. She and Joy Mayfield had dinner the evening before. Joy was happy for her and advised her not to wear too much makeup, since the more naturalistic look was now in vogue. This time, Sandra did not object to the older woman's advice. She went to bed early to wake up refreshed for her 11 o'clock appointment at the modeling agency the following morning. She awoke and had breakfast, then selected an outfit to wear. She chose a simple black and white, form-fitting summer dress – one designed to reveal her curves and accentuate her height. Although the dress was not too fashionable by current New York standards, she hoped it was stylish enough to get her noticed. She took her time to get ready in order to make herself as gorgeous as she possibly could. She called her mother before leaving the apartment. Mary Louise was happy to hear from her and wished her good luck with the appointment. Sandra checked herself in the hallway mirror one last time, grabbed her over-sized, black modeling portfolio, and dashed from the apartment to catch a cab for her 11 o'clock appointment. She gave the taxi driver the address for the modeling agency where she was heading. "160 East 46th Street." The driver pulled up to the entrance a short while later. Sandra paid the fare and then exited the cab. She took the elevator and got off on the 6th floor, and headed straight for the Instant Success Modeling Agency and her 11 o'clock appointment with Ms. Merle Mitchell, the director of the modeling agency. She stepped into the brightly lit office, where she was immediately greeted by the polite welcome of a well-dressed blond receptionist.

"Good morning. May I help you?" the receptionist enquired.

"Yes!" the stunning aspirant replied. "My name is Sandra Davis, and I have an 11 o'clock with Ms. Merle Mitchell."

"Your portfolio, please." Sandra handed the oversized object to the woman. "Have a seat, Ms. Mitchell will see you shortly." Sandra spent the next few minutes leafing through a copy of Vogue Magazine, lying on a coffee table in front of the plush sofa where she sat. The receptionist called out, "Ms. Davis, Ms. Mitchell will see you now. Follow me this way."

She led Sandra down a hallway into a well-lit office where Ms. Mitchell was waiting. Sandra broke out into little rivulets of sweat as waves of anticipation washed over her. The receptionist made the introduction, "Ms. Mitchell, Ms. Sandra Davis," whispering sardonically under her breath, "from Peoria, Illinois."

"Have a seat," said Ms. Mitchell, an imperious-looking woman, fingering a newly teased pile of over-dyed, black hair framing her harsh-looking face. "What can I do for you?"

"Well, I am new to the city," Sandra replied in a somewhat nervous tone of voice. "I was recommended to your agency by a friend of mine back home in Illinois," she spoke hesitantly, as if intimidated by the harsh-looking face posted behind the desk. The kind of face indicative of certain types of business women, particularly the liberated ones who make it their duty to succeed in the male domineering world of New York. Merle Mitchell searched Sandra's face for any signs of flaws. "So you want to be a high fashion model – have you ever modeled before?" Sandra pointed to the portfolio lying in disarray on Merle Mitchell's desk, obviously already scrutinized. "Yes, I can see," the director of the agency replied, seemingly unimpressed by the non-descript quality of the photographs presented in the portfolio. "You still did not answer my question, dear. Have you ever modeled before?" Sandra detected a harsh tone in the business woman's voice.

"Well!" she hesitated. "Once I did a show at J.C. Penny's in the mall back home in Peoria." Merle Mitchell didn't know whether to burst out laughing in Sandra's face or to take her seriously. The imperious-looking owner of the model agency glanced at the fresh-faced farm girl with a sneering look of haughtiness.

"Look, sweetheart," said the woman with the buzzing, beehive pile of over-teased black hair framing her arrogant-looking face, "if you don't have real runway experience, you are only wasting my time. My modeling agency is not a training stable for farm girls from the interior. I don't care how attractive you are. We only deal with the most sophisticated types at this agency." Sandra was devastated by the mean-spirited barrage and the manner in which it was said. She grabbed her portfolio and stormed out of the office, visibly upset, distraught, and downcast but not defeated.

She wandered the streets of New York like a wounded bird, limping on the ground but hoping to soar again. *Surely there are other agencies*, she thought. *I will prove that rotten, hard-nosed, New York, no good bitch, wrong.* She reflected on the treatment meted out to her as nothing more than a bump in the road. She would not let it deter her from her belief in herself or in her dreams. If anything, it would make her more determined than ever to succeed. She was not prepared for such humiliating treatment – the raw reality of it. She did not know such types of people existed in New York – those with the power to deflate the egos of others in such a cruel and mean-spirited manner. *Surely, there will be other opportunities*, she thought. She refused to let herself be suckered in by the undercurrent of such an insensitive and callous soul.

She decided to stop at a coffee shop on Madison Avenue to refresh herself and recover from the blow. She had no idea that New York could be as cruel as that. She thought it was a city where dreams come true, once given the opportunity. She decided to remain as resolute as ever, never for a moment giving in to despair while allowing her survival instincts to kick into high gear. She entered the coffee shop and sat down at a table in a quiet corner, but as soon as she had taken her seat, she immediately felt the weight of eyes staring directly at her from a table across the room. At first, she dismissed it, thinking this could not be true, but the intentional brazenness was aimed directly at her. She tried to avoid looking up for fear of being sucked into the stare, but that only worked for a while. The magnetic power of the aggressiveness, however, continued, causing her to feel a distinct feeling of discomfort and dismay. She thought of her boyfriend, Mark Wilson, and tried to avoid making eye contact with the rudeness of the stare, but that also only worked for a while. The stranger kept up the pressure, which to her seemed indicative of those self-assured, New York types who make it their business to go after what they want.

Sandra felt confused and disoriented by the brazenness of it all. She thought she had no choice but to confront the unexpected rudeness head-on. She edged up slowly, very slowly, until her dazzling green eyes came in contact with that of the stranger's – a handsome, well-built businessman in his mid-twenties – whose raw aggressiveness held her prisoner in a dangerous type of cat-and-mouse game. It only stopped when the stranger got up and walked directly over to her table. Sandra immediately felt befuddled. She thought of the pitfalls that Joy Mayfield had warned her about. *Could this actually be happening to me?* she thought to herself as the uncomfortable scenario continued playing out in front of her. But the stranger had already made his move.

"Hi, may I join you for lunch?" the handsome stranger then introduced himself.

"My name is Eric Flotel. I own a modeling agency here on Madison Avenue, and just could not help staring at your exquisite-looking face. What's your name?" Sandra did not know what to make of the situation. She wondered if this were really true or just some horny New Yorker trying to put the make on her.

What the hell! she thought. *At least, he looks decent to me, plus he owns a modeling agency.*

"My name is Sandra Davis," she replied cautiously.

"I am pleased to meet you, Sandra!" The stranger reached into the breast pocket of the expensive suit he was wearing and pulled out a calling card. He handed it to Sandra who immediately glanced over the glossy object. It read: Eric Flotel, Director, The Flotel Modeling Agency, 690 Madison Avenue, New York, N.Y. 10022; Tel: 212-568-3552. Sandra thought of the card as a prized possession and quickly stashed it away in a purse she was carrying.

The waiter brought over the menu, and they both ordered. "Are you a model?" Eric Flotel enquired. "I see you are carrying a modeling portfolio. May I take a look?" "Sure," Sandra replied.

Eric flipped through the pages and then excitedly exclaimed. "Nice! Nice! I like the one with the wind-blown hair streaking your face." The waiter brought the order and then disappeared. They both picked at their meals while engaging in conversation. "Tell me a bit about yourself," Eric Flotel continued.

Sandra took a sip of her diet coke. "I have recently arrived in the city and am looking for a modeling agency to jump-start my career."

"Look no further," Eric Flotel replied. Sandra thought of the rude treatment recently meted out to her by the director of the modeling agency she had just left.

"When one door closes, another one opens." Eric smiled and opened the door a bit further.

"I like your portfolio very much," he said. "It is very rare to find someone with a look that has such great potential in the modeling world." Sandra Davis ate it up! "I'll be leaving on a business trip tomorrow. I would like to book you for a photo shoot when I return in about a week or two. You have my card. Call and make an appointment. I will tell the receptionist to expect your call." Eric Flotel stared awe-struck into Sandra Davis's incredible green eyes. He buzzed her on the cheek, paid the bill, then walked away. Sandra felt as if she were floating on a cloud. She grabbed her portfolio and dashed excitedly out of the restaurant.

Part V

She was overcome with joy as she blended into the crowd on Madison Avenue in midtown Manhattan. She could not contain herself – such was her excitement she felt in her heart. She hailed a cab to go back to her residence and share the news with those closest to her. She decided against telling her boyfriend Marc Wilson at the present time, fearful it could precipitate a jealous rage on his part, even though he was over a thousand miles away.

She called her mother, who was happy to hear from her but a bit skeptical about the reality of the news. "I don't know what to say, Sandra. I hope it works out well for you."

"Now I will be able to keep the promises I made to you, Mom."

"I will believe it when I see it, honey," her mother replied in a nonchalant way. Sandra waited for Joy Mayfield to return from her office that evening so she could saturate her with tales of her very good luck. "You won't believe what happened to me today, my dear. The appointment at the modeling agency did not work out as planned, but I met this guy in a coffee shop on Madison Avenue. He owns a modeling agency here in the city and even gave me his calling card."

Joy Mayfield listened as Sandra continued excitedly, "He says I have what it takes to be a super model and wants to book me for a photo shoot in the next few weeks. I am so excited; I am about to fly out of my skin."

"Calm down!" Joy said it in a motherly way. "Who is this guy?"

"His name is Eric Flotel, and he runs a modeling agency here in the city. He says I have what it takes to be a big success. Soon I will be bigger than Lauren Hutton and Cheryl Tiegs combined. Just wait and see!"

"That sounds great!" Joy replied. "But how do you know this guy is for real?"

"Well, I just know! He was very impressed with me, and I could tell just by the way he spoke." Joy listened carefully but skeptically and was even a trifle happy for her. "Only in New York, my friend!" she blurted out. "Only in New York!"

Part VI

Sandra called the Flotel Modeling Agency the following day to set up the appointment. The secretary was expecting her call and was extremely polite. She booked her in for Wednesday, August 12th, at 2 p.m., a couple of weeks from the date of Sandra's call. Sandra spent the next two weeks revelling in her newly found fortune, counting down the days to when she would see the handsome stranger again. She also spent time primping and preening, practicing her killer walk for the runway and the photo shoot. She also bought a new outfit for the appointment, straight off the sales rack at Lord and Taylor's Department Store. The weeks sped by faster than she had anticipated, and the day of her appointment had finally arrived. Sandra had spent her time preparing for this moment. She arrived at the appointment looking absolutely dazzling in the slinky outfit she had bought off the sales rack at Lord and Taylor on Fifth Avenue. Eric greeted her with a buzz on the cheek as she sauntered into the modeling agency. He introduced her to the members of the crew. "Hey fellas! This is Sandra Davis, the fabulous young lady I was telling you about. Isn't she – isn't she…" But he never got a chance to complete the sentence. Everyone nodded in agreement with the point he was trying to make.

"Yes! She is sensational!" one associate shouted.

"An absolute knockout!" another exulted.

"Okay, boys! That's enough! Knock it off! Time to get to work!" Eric said to his assembled team.

"Make-up artist!" one assistant shouted.

"Hair dresser," the other called in a high-pitched voice.

The studio professionals went to work, transforming the farm-fresh beauty into someone even more astounding than before. It seemed impossible that anyone could look as sensational as that. Sandra relished the attention, pouting and posing to her heart's content.

"Hold it there!" shouted one photographer. "Give me a cheese cake! Fantastic! Profile!"

"Good!" Sandra was in all her elements. "Give me a sour-face pout. Perfect! Slink a bit, excellent! I will have the contact sheets within a day or two. It was a pleasure working with you, sweetheart." Sandra lapped it up as she sashayed around the photo studio. From that day on, her life would never be the same. She would be transformed from a fresh-faced, naive farm beauty into a sophisticated, high-fashion New York model, with all the fame and glamour expected from such a profession.

Eric was excited by the reception accorded to his latest discovery – the one he encountered purely by chance. He congratulated her on the success of the photo shoot and had her sign a contract, binding her to his agency as well as to he, himself. Sandra revelled in the bliss of the moment and the thought of realizing her most cherished dream. Eric was also pleased and found himself falling under the hypnotic spell of her dazzling green eyes. He even envisioned the advantage of being seen with such a beautiful young creature hanging onto his arms, the type of ornament his associates would certainly be envious of. He subsequently did something totally unexpected – something that also caught her by surprise. "How would you like to have dinner with me this Friday evening?" he said to Sandra.

"Well…" she hesitated.

"Call me as soon as you decide," Eric impatiently said to her.

Sandra left Eric Flotel's fashion agency feeling like a gas balloon floating on air, impatient to share the news with Joy Mayfield, her newly found confidant. She and the older woman had recently become a chummy pair. She took Joy Mayfield to dinner that evening and described in detail the excitement of the photo shoot. She also told her of Eric Flotel's invitation to dinner. "Be careful, Sandra!" the older woman warned her. "Things seem to be moving way too fast. What about your relationship with your boyfriend, Marc Wilson?"

"This is strictly a business deal." Sandra snapped. "Nothing will ever come between Marc and me. Our Mid-

Western roots go back way too far. Eric invited me to dinner because he said he wants me to meet some of his associates in the fashion industry whom he thinks could be very helpful to my career."

"All the same," the older woman replied. "I would be careful if I were you. You never know where such entanglements could lead." Sandra, however, had already made up her mind. She called Eric Flotel the following morning to confirm the dinner appointment for the upcoming Friday evening, 7 p.m., La Roulette, a chic French restaurant on Madison Avenue at 63rd Street on Manhattan's Glamorous Eastside.

All eyes turned as the slinky beauty glided into La Roulette in a white, skin-tight summer dress, revealing every inch and indentation of her luscious curves. Eric chose the restaurant in his well-orchestrated plan to impress and deceive. There were no business associates surrounding him when Sandra waltzed in; only the well-dressed businessman nursing a glass of white wine by himself. He got up and greeted his stunning dinner guest as if he could not get enough of her. After a brief exchange, it suddenly occurred to Sandra that none of the dinner guest that Eric had promised had arrived.

"Where are the associates from the fashion world you said were coming to meet me?" But Eric had the answer well-rehearsed.

"They said if they got delayed, they would meet me at my apartment later for drinks after dinner."

Sandra did not know what to think. She seemed to swallow every word with every sip of her wine. It seemed the crisp white wine and the soft pink lights of the ambience may have gone straight to her head. Eric did the ordering as Sandra poured out the contents of her overly ambitious heart in a desperate attempt to attain her dream. “I will unveil the plan I have in store for you when we get back to my apartment.” Sandra was too glassy-eyed to comprehend the gist of the remark as she continued to climb up the ladder Eric Flotel was providing for her.

Part VII

Eric paid the dinner bill, and they exited the restaurant. Sandra agreed to go with him to his apartment to meet the associates who did not make the dinner appointment. They caught a taxi and headed for the luxury high-rise, located on Third Avenue at 63rd Street, a few blocks north of Bloomingdale’s Department Store. The couple strolled past the doorman arm in arm on their way up to Eric’s apartment on the 22nd floor. Eric opened the door, and they entered. Sandra was immediately bedazzled by the breath-taking view of the New York skyline lit up at night – the magic of its glitter pouring down in the soft moonlight outside.

She felt somehow that she had finally arrived. Eric offered her a drink. He also poured one for himself. “To your success!” He toasted the aspiring beauty. Sandra took a sip, but shortly thereafter started to suffer from a feeling of delayed distress.

“Where are the people you said were coming to meet us here after dinner?”

“I assume they will be here any time now,” the deceptive director replied. But Sandra had become skeptical. She wondered if she had not made a mistake, not realizing she had already fallen into Eric Flotel's trap and which for her was now much too late to avoid. She had already been caught in his inescapable web having falling under his Svengali spell.

Eric offered her another drink, but this time she refused. It seemed to her that the alcohol was now having an unintended effect. It made her appear vulnerable and weak. "I have to go now," she protested, but Eric would have none of it.

"You must believe me when I say to you I am going to make you a super model and a star." Eric detected her downward slide. He reached out and tried to pull her close to him.

"No, Eric!" she shouted. "Stop that. What kind of girl do you think I am?"

"Simply gorgeous!" the deceptive director replied. "I promise I will get you on the cover of every fashion magazine in New York, Vogue: Mademoiselle, Elle, Bazaar, you name it!" But to Sandra, it seemed all he wanted to do was to get her under the designer sheets that covered his bed. He tried to kiss her, but she slapped him in the face. He grinned, as that only riled him up further. This time, he would show her who was in charge. He grabbed her and pinned her against the wall.

"No! Eric!" she pleaded, having lost the ability to resist his advance. He started to undress with the urgency of a man in a hurry to satisfy the lust of his sexual greed. He took off his shirt and started to undress her as well.

Sandra stood next to him in her half-naked state of loneliness and wine, her firm young breasts pointed firmly against the hair of his masculine chest. He led her to the bedroom and finished taking off her clothes. He kissed her once more, more passionately, until they were both consumed by the lava flowing from each other's mouth. They fell onto the bed. He landed on top of her, and they remained entangled in a torrid embrace. He reached over and turned off the light. She felt every sinew of his muscular thighs thrusting against the softness of her satiny flesh. The friction caused a flash of fire between the sheets. And they swayed against each other like a tree caught in the embrace of a sudden thunderstorm. She screamed, and they both exploded into each other like the roar of a mighty waterfall, happily lost in an ecstatic moment of bliss.

They fell asleep, and their dreams intertwined. His hands subconsciously reached for hers in the darkness of the room and overlapped in the crazy jigsaw puzzle of life. They awoke the following morning in the filtered haziness of the sun-drenched room. Eric reached out and pulled her close to him. "You are the girl I've been searching for all my life. Tell me a bit about yourself." Sandra felt guilty and ashamed, knowing she had betrayed the feeling of trust her boyfriend, Mark Wilson, had placed in her, but who was now slowly fading from memory, because of the distances between them and the city in which she now resided and to which she bowed because of the pressures of its demands.

"Well," she hesitated. "I have a boyfriend back home in Illinois," she said, sheepishly, as if in an attempt to regain the upper hand. But her words flowed empty, as the distance of her past, her boyfriend, Marc Wilson and the prospect of her future, Eric Flotel, the one she now lay so comfortably beside, collided like two ships passing in the night in the brutal, unexpected reality of life.

Eric's ego would not allow him the luxury of competition, not even from someone at such vast distances away and who it now seems was lost in the shuffle in the shadows of Peoria, Illinois. "Tell me!" Eric said. "What can he do for you?" Sandra searched hard in the depths of her heart but could not come up with an answer. "Now then," said Eric the Conqueror. "The first part of my plan is to raise your profile by getting you featured on the cover of every fashion magazine in New York. The next thing is for you to be seen in all the right places. I have an invitation for a cocktail party at Bergdorf Goodman, that elegant department store at the corner of Fifth Avenue and Fifty Seventh Street. It is a reception scheduled for early fall for a fashion designer from Rome. That is as good as a place as any for you to start. In the meantime, I would like to take you sight-seeing around the city, if that's okay with you."

"That would be fine!" said the confused, unfaithful, infatuated girl.

Part VIII

Eric felt as if he had just won a prize. He and the green-eyed beauty spent the weekend like newly-mated love birds, kissing and cooing all over New York. He took her shopping, sight-seeing, and lunch at one of the finest restaurants in the city. That Saturday evening, he booked a dinner reservation for two at Tavern on the Green, the iconic New York, touristy restaurant – it's over decorated ambience sparkling like a jewel in Central Park, a magnet for both New Yorkers and tourists alike. Eric and Sandra stepped out of the taxi and were immediately bedazzled by the plethora of Christmas tree lights, decorating the trees and shrubbery in front of the restaurant, from the trunks to the top most branches. It seemed every part of the trees glistened with the sparkling glow of miniature Christmas tree lights, professionally wrapped around every square inch of the trees. The shimmering glow created a mesmerizing effect, reminiscent of a Disneyland ambience in the middle of New York – an enviable glow for the tourists and the privileged of this extraordinary urban wonderland.

After dinner, he took her for a horse-and-carriage ride around Central Park, another of her fantasies fulfilled. It seemed Eric was a genie, granting her every wish. The night simmered with excitement that was just beginning to unfold. After the carriage ride, the pair caught a taxi for disco dancing at the world-famous Regine's, located in the well-heeled Del Monaco Hotel on Park Avenue – the crème de la crème of disco palaces in the city.

Sandra floated into Regine's on Eric Flotel's arm, looking divinely devilish in a red, low-cut, skin-tight disco dress. The photographers surrounded the couple as they waltzed in. Sandra was in all her glory – a real disco queen, a self-absorbed modeling star, shining on the disco scene. The thumping beat of the music sent the disco revelers, rushing to the dance floor as the strobe lights spun their glitter-like magic, bouncing off the shiny surface of the silvery, globular disco balls, spinning above the heads of the patrons. The haunting voice of disco queen Donna Summer summoned everyone to catch the Saturday Night Fever with the number one disco hit, Bad Girls, Talking 'Bout Bad, Bad Girls. Donna Summer's sexy voice delighted all the well-heeled patrons – an international coterie of jet-setters and beautiful people. "That's Candice Bergman!" Sandra swooned over the famous movie star. "And that's Sandra Davis!" Eric, jokingly said to her in all seriousness. "That's whateveryone will be saying when I am finished with my publicity campaign for you."

Part IX

The torrid affair between the rising super model and her benevolent patron, Eric Flotel, suddenly shifted into higher gear. "How would you like to move in with me?" Sandra was pleasantly surprised by Eric's unexpected invitation, which she had not envisioned or expected to be fulfilled. Without giving her a chance to decide, Eric told her he would take her to pick up her suit case at Joy Mayfield's apartment downtown, where she was staying. Joy had told Sandra she would be away for the weekend and would not return until the following Monday evening. The couple drove down to the residence at 160 East 27th Street. Eric waited in his cream-colored Mercedes Coupe as Sandra rushed upstairs to retrieve her suit case. She entered the apartment and quickly penned a note to her absent host.

"Dear Joy," the note began:

"Sorry, I missed you. You did say you would be away for the weekend. I would like to thank you for your hospitality, but I have to let you know, it's time for me to move on.

I will be moving in with Eric Flotel, the director of the fashion agency, who will be handling my affairs from now on. Sorry if I caused you any inconvenience. It's all so sudden and unexpected. Trust you will understand.

Sincerely,
Sandra."

She placed the bombshell on the desk in the living room and put a paper weight on top of it. She gathered her clothes and sundry items and put them in the Samsonite suitcase, then placed the key for the apartment on the desk and rushed back downstairs to Eric, who was waiting for her, snug in his cream-colored Mercedes coupe.

Part X

Joy Mayfield returned from her trip that Monday evening and found Sandra's terse, handwritten note on top of the desk. Her reaction was instantaneous – one of shock and disbelief. At first, she thought it was a joke, but after checking the closet in the hallway, she soon discovered that Sandra's Samsonite suitcase was missing. *I should have known*, the unsuspecting woman said to herself, slowly absorbing the shock of the surprise. It seemed that bitch was not so naive after all. She seemed to be nothing but a user, a cool operator, a woman who will do whatever it takes to get where ever she wants to go in life. Joy folded the note and left it on the desk. *Poor Mark!* she thought. *I don't know how he is going to take this news! I guess my house guest was not that innocent after all.* The distraught woman thought about calling Mark to inform him but decided to wait for the following day after she had recovered from the trip. She awoke the next morning, had breakfast, and shortly thereafter called Marc Wilson. Marc did not take the news very well.

"You shitting me, Joy!" he shouted out in disbelief. "Tell me it's not true!"

"I have the note right here in my hand," Joy replied. "It's the God's honest truth."

"Who is this fucking guy, Eric Flotel? How come I didn't know anything about this before?"

Joy Mayfield thought hard, as if she were keeping secrets for Sandra Davis. "It's as much a surprise to me as it is to you."

"Okay then!" Mark said as he terminated the conversation.

His blood boiled with the fury of the jilted. He reflected on all the things he did to jump-start Sandra's fledgling career: The modeling portfolio he compiled for her, the contact for the modeling agencies he so willingly gave to her and the courage he mustered up to tell her how much he loved her – how much he cared for her, how much he missed her – quite an accomplishment for someone who found it difficult to put his feelings into words. "*Life is not fair!*" Mark Wilson cried to himself; his tears unable to wash away the hurt Sandra Davis caused him. He wandered the streets of Peoria like a wounded animal, robbed of his pride, passion and possession. He vowed, he would find the bitch, the unfaithful one who ditched him for God knows who! He was like a man on a mission who could not live with Sandra's omission from his life. He called Joy a few days later to find out if she had heard from her.

"Not a word," Joy replied, disconsolately.

Mark Wilson spent the next few weeks in Illinois, nursing his grudge. He had also made significant progress pursuing his dreams of becoming a top-notch fashion photographer and his talent was now in much demand, having landed a choice position as an in-house photographer at a fashion conglomerate in Chicago, Illinois. There was even real talk of him becoming as famous as Richard Avedon – the fashion photographer well known in both European and American fashion circles. Joy Mayfield was extraordinarily pleased when Mark Wilson called her one day, not to enquire about Sandra Davis's whereabouts the one who flew the coop, but to tell her that because of his ascending fame as a first rate fashion photographer, he was approached by an art gallery at the Trump Tower, on Fifth Avenue, in New York, and that they had booked him in for an exhibition of his fashion photographs at a gallery there, coincidentally the same week in September as the reception for the Italian, fashion designer, Piero Gallehri at Bergdorf Goodman – the affair Eric Flotel and Sandra Davis were slated to attend.

The reception at Bergdorf Goodman, swung into high gear on the evening of September 15th, 1986. Eric Flotel and his gorgeous model-escort, Sandra Davis, arrived amidst the crush of photographers and the glamorous guests in attendance. Sandra looked incredible in a sexy, blue, Bill Blass designer dress – a seductive little number chosen for her by Eric Flotel from a boutique at Bloomingdales. He thought with a bosom-revealing dress like that, she would be well on her way to becoming the next singular sensation on the New York fashion scene – having her face plastered on the covers of every major fashion magazine in New York and all over the world.

Piero Gallehri, the designer from Rome, stood in the center of Bergdorf's festively decorated fourth floor, holding court, like one of the well-dressed male mannequins in Barney's uptown, Madison Avenue store window.

"Isn't he a peacock for words?" The women guests swooned over the handsome foreigner as if wanting to throw their recently liberated bras at his feet. "Your collection is simply divine, Seignior Gallehri, can't wait to place an order for my next trip south." The guests moved around the room; the way ordinary people moved around the sidewalks of New York City.

Sleekly fitted wasp-waisted waiters, dressed in the black and white uniforms of their professions, sailed back and forth through the thick musical chatter of the room, offering glasses of champagne to the well-heeled guests, while stealing a lecherous look down Sandra Davis's popped up – over-exposed bosom. It seemed the low-cut dress was barely able to contain her overflowing charms. The room suddenly came alive with some of the most powerful and fashionably dressed people in New York City – people famous for one thing or another-wealth, talent, fame and power – you name it. Sandra floated around the room on Eric Flotel's arm – awestruck by the opulence of the festive scene. When he introduced her to the so-called social set, Sandra did her best in trying to impress, offering compliments to one of the glamorous, middle-aged women in attendance. "What a darling little dress, my dear! St. Laurent, isn't it?" The socialite with the puffed-up hair and the over-ripe red mouth walked past Sandra as if the gorgeous one had not spoken at all. The room gushed with an overabundance of phony smiles – Gucci smiles, Armani smiles, Park Avenue smiles – smiles that were the trademarks of people who were experts in the art of bitchiness and guile – people whose dogs and cats probably received diamond collars for Christmas, the way some poor kid in a less privileged area of the city would receive a used teddy bear or a Raggedy Ann, Doll. Sandra thought about the absurdity of it all – the homeless people relegated to sleeping under cardboard boxes in the garish glare of bright street lights – the bag women raiding garbage bins, searching for scraps of existence. This was happening in New York at that time. The contrast jolted her.

"Hold it there!" The photographers snapped as Eric Flotel paraded his latest acquisition around the room – the one not listed on the New York stock exchange. "This is Sandra Davis; the fabulous model I've been telling you about. She is slated to appear on the October cover of Vogue Magazine."

"You mean Vogue Magazine!" one of the guests parroted Eric's remark. Sandra posed and pouted to her heart's content.

"She's also going to be on the cover of Cosmopolitan in a few weeks."

"I can't wait!" one of Eric's associates said.

"You wait!" Eric replied. "Soon, she'll be bigger than Christie Brinkley and Lauren Hutton combined. Now, that's saying a lot." Eric's words flowed smoothly, but it seemed Sandra had had enough. She wanted out – wanted to escape the stifling atmosphere – a room filled with stuffy people whose only commonality was their claim to wealth, power and fame. The contrast between her previous life on the farm and that of her current involvement with New York High Society was particularly jarring to her. Eric checked his watch and realized they had to attend a dinner party at a friend's apartment uptown. He took Sandra by the hand and they both headed for the exit.

"Grazie! Grazie! Thanks for coming! Thanks for coming!" The Italian designer, Piero Gallehri, waved his arms excitedly into the air as Sandra and Eric Flotel, floated away from the gala, festive scene – the phony smiles and the phony guests.

Unbeknownst to the couple as they exited the building, was the fact that Marc Wilson had crossed the street from the Trump Tower where his photographic exhibition had opened a few days before and was now walking up Fifth Avenue on the left-hand side on his way to the Plaza hotel at 58 Street at Fifth Avenue to meet Joy Mayfield and a couple of her friends for drinks. He could not stop thinking about the hurt Sandra Davis had caused him and felt somehow fate would bring them back together again. He was approaching the Fifth Avenue entrance to Bergdorf's, just below the Plaza Hotel when he suddenly saw a couple exiting the store, walking arm in arm, heading up firth Avenue to catch a cab for their dinner party uptown. Mark Wilson did a double take when he saw them. *That woman looks a bit familiar,* he thought. *As a matter of fact, she looks a lot like Sandra Davis. Could that really be?* He followed the couple to make sure it was she and was totally convinced after he recognized that uniquely, provocative walk – that uniquely distinctive walk, a walk he could tell anywhere in the world.

"Life is not fair!" the half-crazed photographer cried. His blood boiled with the fury of the jilted, knowing he had vowed to find the bitch – the unfaithful one who ditched him for someone else. He moved faster to catch up with the couple who had just increased their pace.

"Sandra Davis," he called out in a loud guttural tone, but the couple were too wrapped up in each other, much less to have heard. He increased his pace to make sure they would not get away. "Sandra Davis," he called out again, in a loud rumbling voice – a voice as ominous as that of the roll thunder. Sandra turned and faced him in a shudder of shock and surprise. "Sandra, it's me, Marc, Marc Wilson. Remember me?" Sandra froze when she recognized her former flame from Peoria, Illinois – the one she had so heartlessly deserted. Marc Wilson quietly reached into the pocket of the trench coat he was wearing and pulled out a concealed gun he was carrying. He aimed the weapon directly at Sandra Davis's flawless face, then pulled the trigger – releasing all his pent-up anger and rage. He watched as she fell like a tree in a forest – falling in slow motion onto the sidewalk of New York in front of Bergdorf Goodman's Department Store, fatally wounded. Eric Flotel stood and stared like a statue in a state of shock and total disbelief.

Marc Wilson dropped the gun and walked away. He did not get far, however. He was quickly apprehended by a pair of New York City police officers who were patrolling in the area and who quickly wrestled him to the ground. A commotion ensued and a huge crowd quickly gathered in front of Bergdorf Goodman's on Fifth Avenue. The night sky was instantly lit up by the flares of flashing lights from police cars and the wail of an ambulance that had arrived on the scene shortly thereafter. Marc Wilson was roughed up by the police, placed in handcuffs, and taken away in a police cruiser. Sandra Davis's body was covered up by a white sheet, placed on a gurney, sailed into the back of a coroner's van then driven away in a different direction. The incident even made the 10 o'clock news that night. The reporter Melanie McGhee of Channel Five News, reported live from the scene in front of Bergdorf Goodman. "Mid-Western Model Murdered in Mid-Town Manhattan, photographer boyfriend arrested."

Eric Flotel was too shaken up to give a statement to the Police. He had to be taken to the Lennox Hill Hospital to be treated for severe shock and trauma – as he was unable to contemplate a future without the one in whom he had invested so much – the one well on her way to becoming the first international modeling superstar, whose only objective was to achieve success in the competitive world of high fashion modeling. A liberated young lady who wanted to have it all.

Within a matter of hours, Marc Wilson had attained the notoriety and fame that had so far eluded his former flame

– Sandra Davis – a woman whose only objective was to achieve success in her chosen career, no matter the cost. She was a woman brave enough to take on the challenges of a city like New York while ignoring the pitfalls that awaited her along the way to fame. It was unfortunate that she had to pay the ultimate price for not playing by the rules of loyalty and faithfulness demanded by the one who previously helped her along the way. The following morning, Marc Wilson's face was splashed across the front page of every major newspaper in New York – all except the flashy, fashion magazines, Vogue, Cosmopolitan and Elle and Bazaar.

Lydia My Love

(A Love Story Set in Pre-Independent Jamaica)

Part I

Lydia, for lack of a more rational explanation, seemed to be a girl adrift in a world of her own, lost and alone as if trapped in a twilight zone, although surrounded by other family members – two sisters, a youthful-looking father, and a stern, overly protective mother. She did not relate well to her sisters – a situation that was probably caused by the competitive nature of sibling rivalry. She was a girl as fragile as a flower, one whose petals were just now beginning to open into the full bloom of life. She sometimes appeared to be drifting in and out of a twilight zone – fully focused at times – introspective and withdrawn on other occasions. It was a situation over which it seemed she had no control. Although at once beautiful and desirable, it appeared something of a disturbing nature was surely amiss. She was a girl who at times was given over to fits of a melancholy mood. What factors drove her melancholia? Quite possibly she herself did not know. Yet the thing hovered over her like an unwanted nightmare, tormenting her psyche, disturbing her soul like a bad case of teenage angst.

Neither of her two sisters, Jean and Joan Flynn, could boast the advantage of Lydia's striking good looks, as a result, they formed a bond of resentment against her, one which only further widened the wedge of their rivalry, causing them to shut her out of their conversations or just be plain rude to her. She never felt close to or that she could confide in them.

Fortunately, her appealing good looks gained her the attention of many secret admirers, particularly the teenage boys in her neighborhood – those vying for the opportunity to get close to her. Lydia used her dreamy brown eyes to captivate or make a captive of anyone falling prey to her enigmatic persona. The boys in her neighborhood secretly slugged it out among themselves like little love-starved soldiers, vying for the privilege of gaining her attention, almost as if engaged in warfare on a battlefield of love.

Igall Flynn, Lydia's father was an officer in his country's defense force, a forceful though jovial man, somewhere in his mid-forties. He was blessed with a flash bulb smile whose photographic intensity the fortunate Lydia had also inherited. He was the foundation of her life– the rock upon which her hopes and dreams were built – the only one in the family to whom she felt somewhat close. But all that changed after he was conscripted for military service overseas by the lieutenant in charge of his country's defense force, The Royal Regiment of Jamaica. The lieutenant had selected him for that special assignment in London, England, because of his valor, discipline and military expertise.

In contrast to her husband, Caroline Flynn, the mother of his three teenage daughters, was a woman of a more somber disposition. She was a teacher at St Hughs, one of the island's leading secondary schools. She was a strict disciplinarian – a woman with beady brown eyes, half closed from too many years of visual reprimand. Because of her husband's overseas deployment, Mrs. Flynn had decided to raise her daughters in a strict, no-nonsense manner, like the proverbial mother hen, under the dark and stifling shade of her wings. From now on, she and she alone would be responsible for their upbringing. She had lately become concerned with the pressing problems facing the mother of every teenage girl: the problems of dating, premarital sex, and outright rebelliousness. She was familiar with the horror stories being bandied about, concerning the unwanted pregnancies, secret house parties, and total disregard for parental control. As a result, she had vowed to protect their reputation while their father was away, far from his island base, on military service in a foreign land. She was fearful of having their names batted about like ping pong balls from the mouth of one neighbor to another – that was something she would not tolerate, not in the close-knit community in which she evolved. No one whom she did not know would be allowed to visit the house. That was her finite unbreakable rule.

Fortunately for me, one of Lydia's most ardent admirers, I was automatically excluded from that restrictive consideration – the fact that Lydia's parents and mine were neighbors and good friends. This gave me the advantage of visiting Lydia whenever I desired. As a result, I quickly became the envy of the boys in the neighborhood, particularly those yearning for a chance to get close to Lydia. “Tell me, Logan,” they often accosted me on the street. “We always see you hanging around Lydia’s house. What is she like? Did you ever kiss her?”

“What’s that to you?” I fired back, but instead of placating them, it seemed my answer only served to further pique their curiosity.

“Did you ever see her in her bra?”

“That’s none of your business!” I snapped back at them.

Although blessed with a uniquely beautiful face, Lydia somehow managed to remain unaffected by the advantage of her stellar good looks. Her two sisters were also attractive, though no one paid much attention to them when she was around. Lydia stood five feet six inches tall, with flowing black hair crowning an exquisite-looking face. She had light brown eyes protected under arches of long, black brows, and her cheeks were slashed by a delightful – pair of dimples which exposed exquisitely shaped ivory teeth whenever she smiled. Although I enjoyed being around all three sisters, my interest was reserved primarily for the mysterious Lydia. Something about her intrigued me – something that brought out the Columbus in me.

This inducement was due not only to her beauty but also a perplexing aspect of her enigmatic persona. This I found quite troubling because it forced me to reflect upon the various occasions when she would become sadly reflective and a strange and faraway look would suddenly creep into her eyes. This made her seem as if she had drifted off into a twilight zone. Then, as if realizing she was still in the midst of the company of others, she would quickly snap out of that mode and suddenly be herself once more.

I observed this troubling aspect of her emotional state on more than one occasion when my brothers and I would stop by to visit Lydia and her sisters after school. We would quickly rush home, change our school uniforms, and then dash over to Lydia's house as quickly as we could. It was always a happy occasion when we visited with her and her sisters. We would play cards, tell jokes, or just hang around having a jolly good time. Sometimes, when we became too boisterous and the noise spun recklessly out of control, Mrs. Flynn, in her authoritative role as a parent, would suddenly interrupt and admonish us sternly, "Keep it down, kids. You are making way too much noise!" On other occasions, she would be a dear and bring us huge servings of Jell-O and ice cream, her favorite dessert. She was always fond of serving tea, British style, at four o'clock in the afternoon. This gave her the opportunity to show off her fine bone china, in which she served us tea using the new Lipton flow – through teabags. After tea was served, she would disappear and would not resurface until the noise once again spun out of control.

Having become accustomed to our presence at the house, Mrs. Flynn invited my brothers and me to have dinner with the family one Sunday afternoon. It was a gesture we appreciated – one we looked to with exaggerated anticipation. After a delicious meal of roast chicken and rice and peas, Mrs. Flynn invited us to stay and play a game of monopoly with her girls. The passionate nature of the game once again led to another boisterous outburst, which caused Mrs. Flynn's parental instincts to instantly kick into high gear – just at the time it had started to turn dark. With a stern look on her face, she once again issued her unchallenged directive. “Time to run along, Sonnies. Make sure to get home before it gets dark.” It seemed she had an unfounded fear that something perverse would happen to her daughters if we stayed after dark. We left, but reluctantly.

Part II

From what I had gleaned just hanging around Lydia, it seemed something of a disquieting nature was bothering her, but that she had no one in whom to confide, not her mother or her sisters. No one at all! This made her appear distant and out of touch, as if she were focusing completely within herself. I remembered the different occasions while visiting when the same strange out of touch look would suddenly creep into her eyes forcing me to wonder why she occasionally seemed so out of touch. I wondered what could be causing her such distress. Then I thought to myself, *why should a girl as beautiful as she be so tortured from within?* The answer to this question would be revealed in the pages ahead.

One afternoon while visiting without my brothers, Lydia asked me to stay a bit longer to help her with her homework. We were sitting on the front veranda when suddenly she turned to me with a strange and quizzical look in her eyes. “Tell me, Logan!” she ventured softly. “Have you ever been awakened out of your sleep at night by a terrifying nightmare?” The nature of the question caught me by surprise and left me wondering what this was all about.

"Gee, Lydia!" I said, trying not to sound too surprised. "I don't know what to say. I don't think I've ever had an experience like that."

"Let's drop the subject," she said abruptly. "You will be happy to know I am thinking about majoring in psychology when I go to college."

"Psychology!" I said in surprise.

"Yes!" she answered. "Wouldn't you like to know the reason people do the things they do?"

"I guess so," I said, not wanting to push the subject further.

The quirky nature of the question suggested to me that she was trying to discover the reason for whatever was bothering her. She then rambled on to a different topic. "You will be happy to know I have developed an interest in the study of spiders."

"That's interesting!" I said with a feeling of concern, thinking how weird a subject. I assumed her interest was a spillover from her biology class at school. She informed me that she was assigned the task of collecting spiders by her biology teacher as a school project and then asked me to accompany her on a field trip to the botanical gardens to collect the specimens needed for her project.

After getting her mother's approval, we decided to meet the following Sunday for the trip to the Hope Botanical Gardens, a virtual nature paradise situated at the foothills of the cool Blue Mountains on the outskirts of the city of Kingston. There, in the compacted conglomeration of exotic trees, she would find all the spiders needed for her assignment.

I picked her up that following Sunday afternoon at about one o'clock for the trip to the botanical gardens. Lydia looked lovely in a lacy lavender dress. I complimented her on how beautiful she looked. She blushed and aimed that flash bulb smile at me, exposing those exquisitely shaped ivory teeth. My heart raced with excitement. We headed for the bus stop a short distance from her house and caught the number six bus for the trip to the Hope Botanical Gardens. We arrived at our destination after a pleasant ride and headed straight for the avenue of the tree-lined street which led to the entrance of the gardens. I took Lydia's hand in mine; she didn't seem to mind. We walked and talked about things relevant to our teenage lives; at that juncture, she did not seem too interested in the study of spiders. I felt a rush of excitement just looking at her and fantasized about kissing her each time we passed under the umbrage of a thick growth of trees. Such was the ambience of this lush, paradisiacal landscape – a garden rich with the perfume of exotic tropical blooms, infusing the air with the scent of their delicate perfume. Among these were wild orchids, roses and the blue fox glove – Lydia in search of spiders, while I was looking for love.

We found a few trees with the intricate design of spider webs attached. Lydia excitedly poked the critters out of their domain and slid them into a perforated matchbox carried expressly for that purpose. But even after the box was filled and the lid securely fastened into place, it seemed she could not stop staring at the center of the web. She seemed fascinated in a strange, inexplicable way. Could it be that she identified with the spiders because she also felt herself caught in a web – the web of small-town existence with all the attendant problems inflicted upon everyone – the gossip and innuendos, neighbors spying on each other, people planting hedges to protect their privacy? I turned over this question in my mind the way one would a stone on a freshly mowed lawn, only to find a moist, under-exposed side.

After collecting the critters, we rushed to catch the bus for the return trip home. Lydia thanked me for accompanying her, stating that her mother hardly allowed her out of the house. *How absurd*! I thought, 17 years old and sequestered like that! She suddenly turned and looked at me with a tinge of sadness in her eyes. I wondered if that twilight zone look was about to descend upon her once more. It seemed that the overly protective manner in which Mrs. Flynn was rearing her daughters was probably the contributing cause of Lydia's emotional distress – a psychological tug-of-war between wanting to obey her mother's strict rules or yield to the innate stirrings of her feminine desires. I wondered if Mrs. Flynn was aware of Lydia's dilemma. If she were, she did not seem concerned at all.

Part III

One night while visiting, and after her mother and sisters had retired to bed for the night, Lydia and I sat on the beige sofa in the living room, where I was helping her with her homework. The radio hummed softly in the background as the full moon cast its cold, pale light through the living room window and onto the recently polished floor. A melancholy look once again washed over her face, making her appear sad and withdrawn. It was the same troubling expression I had observed on her face so many times before and which forced me to have a feeling of great concern for her. Lydia suddenly leaned forward as if wanting to say something, but withdrew again just as quickly. She fidgeted with the pages of her biology book, opening and closing it over and over again. It became apparent, something disconcerting was bothering her, but that she found it difficult to disclose. She then abruptly said to me, "Logan, let's call it quits."

"Call what quits?" I asked, afraid she was referring to my frequent visits to the house.

"The homework," she answered.

"Oh!" I said, breathing a sigh of relief, feeling happy that she was not referring to my frequent visits to the house.

She then continued, "It's just that – It's just that." but she could not bring herself to reveal what it was she wanted to say.

"What's the matter, Lydia," I said enquiringly.

She then lowered her head and softly turned toward me. "It's just that…it's just that –" yet she could not bring herself to reveal what it was; she just could not say.

"Come on, Lydia," I prodded her, my impatience getting the better of me.

"Why can't you say what you have to say?" She quickly tossed her biology book aside as a stream of tears welled in her eyes. "It's just that I can't concentrate," she finally said. "I don't know what's wrong." She then buried her head against my shoulder. "Logan!" she continued, as a torrent of tears welled in her eyes.

“Never reveal to anyone what I am about to say to you.” I gave her my word of honor, crossed my heart, etc. However, I could not help but wonder what could be causing her such distress.

“Please bear with me,” she continued. “This isn’t easy!” She finally composed herself and bravely continued, “Logan!” she sobbed. “I have been suffering from a terrible recurring nightmare that has just about destroyed my peace of mind, haunting me during the day and which causes me to be fearful at night. Worse yet, it even makes me feel afraid of going to sleep.”

She related that as she slept, she would envision herself being attacked by ferocious bird-like creatures with massive beaks and strong, heavy claws that would suddenly swoop down upon her during her sleep and then proceed to gorge out huge chunks of her flesh; that when she tried fending them off, the grotesque creatures would suddenly make loud jeering sounds that caused her to wake up frightened, afraid of going back to sleep. I listened as the confidential tears rolled down her cheeks. *Poor, Lydia!* I thought. That explains why she so often drifted off into those dangerous daydreams when she would stare expressionlessly into the deep distance of space as if her eyes were devoid of vision.

The horror story freaked me out and filled me with a real feeling of concern for her. It seemed the cloistered manner in which Mrs. Flynn was rearing her teenage daughters, was probably responsible for Lydia’s psychoses – the inner turmoil she was now experiencing. The tale of her distress suggested to me that some repressive force had taken control of her life, contributing to the terrifying nightmares.

I put my arms around her to comfort her. “Don’t worry, Lydia,” I said to her. “From now on, everything is going to be alright. You don’t have to be concerned anymore. I’ll be there for you.” I held her tightly as a soft rain of tears trickled down her cheeks. Lydia glanced up at me with her tear-stained eyes, which flickered with a sudden look of awareness and surprise. I felt guilty about the circumstances, but I immediately realized that we were falling in love.

“Baby, it’s you!” An oldie by the Shirelles, spun from the radio humming softly in the background. I held her tightly and felt her warmth against my chest while gently kissing away her tears.

Everything suddenly became one big blur, as if the world itself was spinning out of control. Such was the feeling of happiness I felt in my heart. Lydia now appeared more relaxed and passionately responded to my embrace. She looked into my eyes as our lips moved closer and closer until we were locked into a liquid embrace. A chilling feeling warmed my heart as we remained wedged into each other’s arms and into each other’s visions of dizzying emotions. How strange and beautiful the world had suddenly become! I started to dream, and it seemed for the first time that Lydia could also dream without fear of having it interrupted by those dreadful nightmares. I felt happy knowing that we now had each other. “Lydia!” I whispered. “I have always been in love with you. You may not have known, but I sensed what we’re going through.” We kissed and kissed until our lips were no longer starved for love.

“I always knew you were the only one I could confide in,” she said softly. “The only one who understood what I was going through.”

That night, the magic of love transformed us both. Lydia told me she no longer felt fearful of the nightmares or even going to sleep. I felt a great feeling of relief, both for her and for myself. I assured her that I would always be there for her and that things would be different from now on. She smiled at me as if to confirm that her nightmares were finally over. I dreaded the thought of leaving her that night, but I rejoiced in the fact that I had reason to celebrate. I asked her out on a date, not thinking of the formidable opposition I expected from her mother. However, by now Mrs. Flynn had grown accustomed to my presence at the house. She gave us her blessings, which helped to smooth things out. In the ensuing months, we went on many dates together – movies, house parties, beach picnics, even a trip back to the botanical garden, where I first fantasized about kissing her as we walked under the leafy shade of the overhead trees. Our love blossomed, and it seemed the lovely Lydia was also in bloom – more radiant and lovelier than I could ever remember. We looked forward to the day when we would get married. Such was the happiness we felt in our hearts. It seemed our future together loomed brighter than the light of the full moon reflected on the recently polished floor of the living room. We looked forward to the day when we would announce our engagement while envisioning a future for ourselves – a house in the country filled with the fiery laughter of children at play.

Such happiness seemed almost impossible to bear. I wondered if this were real!

However, it seemed all those ambitious dreams and schemes were nothing but fantasies slated never to be. Lydia called me one afternoon and asked me to come over to the house, stating she had something to tell me. I was happy because she wanted to see me, but I could not figure out what kind of news she had in store for me. I rushed over to the house later that afternoon. We kissed as she greeted me in a stylish casual outfit. She then aimed that flash-bulb smile at me, melting my heart. She offered me a drink, and we both sat down on the sofa.

"What's up, Lydia?" I said, waiting for her to spring the news. She just smiled and kept on smiling. "Okay, Lydia," I said. "Let's have it!" She then composed herself and looked me directly in my eyes; by then I was overcome with a feeling of anxiety. She then related that her mother had received an important communiqué from the lieutenant in charge of her father's military base in London, informing her that her father had been rewarded with a significant promotion in the British Foreign Service because of his extraordinary competence, valor and military expertise. I was relieved and very happy to hear the news, and I congratulated her on her father's behalf. She accepted with a warm hug and a kiss. I, however, was soon to discover, that that was not the end of the surprise. I thought I myself would start having nightmares when Lydia looked me directly in the eyes and sprang the biggest surprise I have ever had in my life. She informed me that in a matter of weeks, she, her mother, and her sisters would be leaving the island to join their father at his military base in the cold, white dampness of London.

On a Positive Note

(An Intriguing Saga)

Photo courtesy of Keanne van de Kreeke

The day emerged on a positive note, sunny, bright, and unmistakably clear. The sunrise had the power to mesmerize. It seemed one could spend the entire morning staring at its compelling beauty. It was a sight that warmed the heart and soothed the soul – nourishment for both physical and spiritual well-being. Suddenly, however, the clouds moved in, obliterating the sunlight and the feelings of euphoria associated with it. Rain threatened, but by mid-morning, the sky had recovered. The sun peered through, chasing away the debilitating dreariness while simultaneously transforming the sky into a magnificent shade of blue – no ordinary blue either, but one as uncompromisingly lovely as that of the delicate hues embedded into the patterns of fine porcelain China. Little white puffs of clouds appeared then magically morphed into various and interesting animalistic shapes as perceived by one's imagination. The flow of light emanating from the clouds shone with a reflected glory so bright, it had the unintended effect of hurting one's eyes. A mild breeze stirred the Dagwood trees, hastening the flight of birds circling lazily above the landscape.

It was a day in spring when everyone felt resurrected, grateful for the chance of being brought back to life. It had been a cold and cruel winter, one plagued with lingering memories of a specialized viciousness – such was the scenario in the aftermath caused by a series of wicked winter storms. Everywhere one looked, one would see evidence of the damages: debris scattered on front lawns everywhere. Ornamental trees uprooted from their moorings in the ground. Giant oaks and other leafy shade trees saturated with the burden of fractured limbs and broken branches. Roads in the area had also taken a beating – their surface scarred and disfigured by innumerable ugly-looking potholes, while on the main streets of town one would encounter the same sad, beleaguered-looking faces of winter-ravaged people.

However, this beautiful, spring-like day was a day to celebrate, a day to appreciate the loveliness of outdoor life – a day for hiking, biking, jogging, gardening, etc. It was the perfect day for everyone and anyone who appreciate the freedom of being outside.

Larry London, an established resident of Phillipsfield, Connecticut, was also inspired by the magical spell cast by this uniquely beautiful, post-winter day. He revelled in the feelings of well-being it afforded him, a budding artist, a lover of outdoor life. He was out for his usual morning walk when suddenly he was struck by the calculated force of an unexpected revelation, the thought of how lucky some people are, especially those fortunate enough to be able to enjoy a day such as this, people unencumbered by the constraints of a nine-to-five existence, those who remain unaffected by the dreary routine of life.

Luckily for Larry, he could be counted among the fortunate few: an artist by profession, a painter of landscapes, still life, flowers, etc. Among his other talents was his gift as a pianist. He occasionally indulged his love of music by occasionally tinkering with the bi-colored keys of his beloved piano, a Steinway Grand, a gift inherited from his father, a pianist of note. Because of the provenance of the instrument, Larry made sure that it would occupy a position of prominence in the library of his Connecticut country home. The Steinway was a treasure which he appreciated more than any other of his prized possessions, never for a moment stopping to think that one day, that very instrument would play (if you will excuse the pun) a prominent role in the life of a total stranger – a saga which, due to divine providence and the mellifluous notes of the Steinway, would have the good fortune of ending on a positive note.

Larry London’s house in Phillipsfield was established on a choice plot of land in the envied quietude of the

Connecticut countryside. The site, chosen for its privacy and remoteness, was surrounded by hundreds of acres of forested land, a great portion of which was deeded over to recreational open space by a wealthy philanthropist of Phillipsfield as a gift for all the local residents to enjoy. The house was located on a long, narrow stretch of country road, which ran roughly about a mile into the woods. The edifice was made of fieldstones and glass, which gave the structure its look of solidity, its character, and its charm. In the remoteness of its location, it could be compared to the iconic structure, Wuthering Heights, as celebrated in British Literature by its author, Emily Bronte – an isolated residence plunked down into the lush green loveliness of the Connecticut countryside. Although prized for its privacy and remoteness, the peaceful ambience was occasionally broken by the noise of single-engine air planes from the nearby airport in the adjoining town, circling noisily above and unsettling the nerves of the residents below.

In the novelty of its location, Larry found peace and inspiration for all his creative endeavors, and on a day as inspiring as this, he decided to take his easel outdoors to paint 'en 'plein air. After a successful stint on the canvas, he decided it was time to take a break. *What better way to relax,* he thought, than by tinkling with the black and white keys of his beloved Steinway! A piano is not an instrument to be ignored; its presence, like that of a beautiful woman, demands attention, a necessity to be reinforced – celebrated if you may by the touch of human hands, in this case, the talented touch of Larry London's sensitive hands. He positioned himself at the piano and then began to play. First, he ran the scales before proceeding to the melodies of his favorite Broadway show tunes: Les Misérables, Phantom of the Opera, and The Sound of Music, etc. As he massaged the tactile keys of the piano, the mellifluous notes of the Steinway joyfully floated away, like pebbles cast upon the surface of a musical pond, sending ripples of vibration cascading throughout the vast expanse of the wooded wonderland surrounding his home and far beyond.

Because of the ideal springtime weather, other residents of Phillipsfield had also decided to venture outdoors into the open arms of the open space, some for the therapeutic value of the woods, others for adventure and the challenges of exploring the rugged nature trails. Larry London continued playing, having become lost in the glorious sound of his own music-making, unaware that on the opposite side of town, a group of boy scouts and their scout master had set out on an expedition into the sacred heart of the reverential woods, a significant distance from his residence on the opposite side of town.

The woods of the open space served as a great attraction for all kinds of adventure seekers. The scout master in charge, most assuredly, was aware of that fact. Many were the expeditions he had led into the tangled heart of these rugged woods. He was familiar with the challenges of the terrain – the unexpected hazards and dangers. He knew every twist and turn, every obstacle waiting around the bend. He had earned his stripes! He was aware that in the interior one would encounter many unusual and interesting sights, particularly the breath-taking rock formations from the Glacial Epoch, many of which were covered with all types of lichens and dark green moss which gave the rocks a decided look of timelessness and added immeasurably to their aged presence.

There were also crystal-clear streams meandering through the sun-lit landscape – a place where deer and other wildlife often congregated to have a cooling drink or just relax. The sights became even more interesting as one ventured further into the interior. There one would discover the thick, green growth of hemlock pines, plus a vast array of other forested trees: The Mighty Oaks, Silver Birch, Tulip Trees, even the sickly-looking Gray Ash Tree, recently placed on the endangered list.

An abundance of wildlife also made this domain their home; these included raccoons, possums, beavers, woodchucks, chipmunks, snapping turtles, plus herds of tawny-colored deer running wild. Here in the quietude of these woods, one would also encounter the poisonous and scary-looking diamond-backed copperhead snakes, many of which lived under these ancient rocks. There were also purportedly old Indian burial mounds, as referred to in the novel The Last of the Mohicans by author James Fenimore Cooper, all of which helped to form an integral part of Phillipsfield's historic lore.

As Larry London played with abandon, the hills surrounding his home suddenly came alive with the sound of music – his own music-making, which echoed joyously throughout the hills and valleys surrounding his home and which filtered out into the woods of the open space. Could it be that the trees in the woodlands of the open space were also listening to the music? That would not be surprising – such was the beauty of the mellifluous notes floating away from the Steinway. It seemed the more Larry played, the more lost he became in the music – a fact which rendered him almost incapable of hearing the sound of any other noise.

Suddenly, however, there was a knocking at the backdoor to his residence, all be it a sound too faint for him to have heard. Larry continued playing unperturbed. Shortly thereafter, there was another knocking sound, a bit stronger than the first, but nothing that would be disruptive or cause concern. However, a few seconds later, there was a much louder knocking sound, one that could be heard above the music of the piano. Larry also heard it but remained unperturbed, too wrapped up in the music of the show tunes to be disturbed. *Must be the wind interfering with the screen door to the kitchen,* he thought, *or maybe it could be the mailman, who occasionally brought the mail to the house.* However, being late afternoon, he knew it was way past delivery time. Larry remained focused only on the melodies of the show tunes and the magical sound of the Steinway. Finally, however, there was an intrusively loud banging sound at the back door to his property, one whose urgency of purpose he could no longer ignore. It was a sound so loud it finally scored. *"Bam, bam, bam, bam, bam."* This time it got Larry's attention. He immediately jumped up from the piano and rushed toward the back door leading to the kitchen to investigate.

He opened the door, then stood and stared in total disbelief. There on the landing leading to the kitchen door, stood a boy, a disheveled little boy, about 12 years old, with tears streaming down his frightened-looking face as he tried his best to fight back tears. The sight of the youngster startled Larry, who did not know what to make of such a bizarre situation unfolding at his door.

"Who are you?" he demanded of the youngster. "What's the matter? Why are you crying?" But he was not prepared for the answer that ensued.

"I am a boy scout," the youngster sobbed. "I was late in meeting up with my scouting buddies after my mom dropped me off at the entrance to the open space on the other side of town, a significant distance from your property here. She dropped me off at the place where we were supposed to meet up.

"Apparently, because she was late, my buddies left without me. I went looking for them but instead got lost. I then found myself wandering through the vastness of the woods, scared and alone, wondering if I would ever find my way back home. I kept on walking for a very long time, dazed and confused when suddenly I heard what sounded like music in the woods, but I wondered if I wasn't imagining things. However, I kept on walking briskly toward the direction of the sound while searching for my buddies. The closer I got, the more real the music sounded. It then became apparent that it was someone playing a piano. I was immediately overcome by a feeling of relief knowing there would be someone there to help. I then started running faster and faster until I finally found myself here, on the doorsteps to your house."

Larry's face registered a look of shock as he absorbed the impact of the frightening tale. "O my God!" he exclaimed.

"What an incredible ordeal for any youngster to endure. Are you okay?" the little scout asked for a glass of water.

Larry quickly obliged, seeing how pale and dehydrated the youth appeared. The youngster gulped down the water then thanked his host.

“What’s your name?” Larry enquired.

“Peter Anderson,” the boy replied.

“Do you know your telephone number, Peter?” The little scout gathered himself, stood at attention as if to regain his lost composure, and then rattled off the number as quickly as he could. Larry dialed. The voice of a woman at the other end of the line answered.

“Mrs. Anderson?” he enquired.

“Yes?” the woman replied, hesitantly.

“My name is Larry London,” he continued. “I live here on High Mountain Road in Phillipsfield, and have here with me a little boy by the name of Peter Anderson.”

“Did you say Peter Anderson?” the woman asked frantically.

“Yes!” Larry replied.

“That’s my son,” the woman said. “Is he okay?”

“Yes!” Larry answered. “May I speak to him?”

“Just a minute!” Larry handed the phone to the boy.

“Hi, Mom,” said Peter, in a quivering tone of voice. “Are you okay, Honey?”

“Yes, yes, Mom,” the little scout’s voice quivered. “After you dropped me off, I went in search of my scouting buddies, but soon discovered they had left without me. I went looking for them, but instead got lost.”

“Don’t worry, sweetheart,” said the boy’s mother in a comforting tone of voice. “Mommy will be over to get you right away.” The boy handed the phone back to Larry, who promptly gave the woman directions to his house.

Larry and the boy then stepped outside to wait for his mother on the brick terrace pavement next to the asphalted driveway. The youngster now appeared more relaxed and composed, knowing his mother was on her way and that he would soon be going home.

Within half an hour's interval, a blue Volvo Station Wagon pulled into the driveway of Larry London's country home. The woman parked the car, hurriedly got out, then rushed frantically toward her son standing by the driveway. The boy joyfully opened his arm as his mother rushed toward him. The scene was as heart-rending as that of the ending of any Hollywood movie. Larry stood aside and watched the dramatic climax – the hugs, kisses, and tears of a mother and child's reunion and was also overcome by the intensity of its emotional impact. The woman thanked him, gathered her precious little cargo, and quickly sped away down the narrow country road.

Larry recovered and breathed a sigh of relief, grateful that the little scout's ordeal was finally over, and that he was now heading back to the safety of his mother's home, where he rightfully belonged. He reflected on the incident, which he considered nothing more than an interrupted interlude, the unknown factors which can so readily and unexpectedly interfere with the regular flow of daily life. He marveled at how fortunate the boy was to have heard the music emanating from the piano, and which gave him hope and comfort while wandering through the woods, lost and alone. He thought of the dangers the little scout could have encountered, both from unknown factors and those inherent within the boundaries of the open spaces of the woods. He felt an overwhelming feeling of satisfaction knowing that he did all he could in helping to bring the scout's ordeal to a successful conclusion.

He then walked back inside the house to the patiently waiting Steinway, sat down on the over-varnished wood bench, and gently stroked the keys, as if to let the piano know how much it was appreciated and the very important role it played in bringing the scout's ordeal to a happy end. He reflected on the incident, rejoicing at how fortunate the boy was to have heard the music of the piano reverberating throughout the woods of the open space and which led him directly to a place where he could finally get help. Larry marveled at the fact that what could have become a tragic tale for the lost scout and the traumas he endured, instead, thanks to divine providence and the mellifluous notes of the Steinway – it all had the good fortune of ending on a positive note.

Portrait of My Mother

It has been many years since my mother quietly made her exit from this world. The intervening period gave me the time to reflect upon her life and all she meant to me. The following words always accompanied her throughout her life: Mommy, Mama, Mom – a variation of different appellations for the same lady – the first words uttered by an infant in recognition of the face that would be the most familiar during the course of its lifetime.

I slowly got to know my mother – the woman who gave birth to me – the one who brought me into this world. I had no recollection of that fact being only a baby at that time. However, I imagined how fondly I gazed up into her eyes during my infantile state while she breast-fed me – her new-born child, the way she previously shared her warmth and sustenance with my older brother and sister.

My mother was a kind, caring and loving soul. God bless her heart! As I matured I got to know her and realized just how fortunate I was to have had her as my mom. She always wore a beautiful smile while twirling her widow's peak – the V-shaped tuft of hair that stood out prominently on her forehead and was one of her most recognized features. The expressive openness of her smile indicated she was happy being a mother – a guiding light to all her children – my brothers, my sisters and me. She made sure I would have enough playmates to keep me happy as well as to torment me – all part of the learning process in dealing with and coping with others in life. We loved each other although we also had our fights. Such were the challenges of growing up with a plethora of playmates especially when it came to navigating the minefields of life. This was especially true whenever my siblings and I indulged in playing games of cards or monopoly knowing no one wanted to be the loser. My mother always ended up being the referee when our father was not around to enforce his particular form of discipline – a fact we resented at that time, but which we learned to appreciate in later life.

My mother's life could be considered a monument to motherhood. I would easily erect such a structure to honor her memory. Her nurturing qualities were as natural as she was – qualities stamped in the DNA of her soul – Defend her children – Never allow them to go astray – Always care for them. This philosophy guided her in raising exceptional children, all of whom became accomplished in their own particular fields of endeavor. Mama was an exceptional woman, beloved and respected by all her children – all vying to gain her love and attention in what sometimes devolved into the arena of sibling rivalry, a situation that I discovered was better left alone – best left unsaid – such is the power of silence.

We were reared in different times – in the Jamaica of the nineteen fifties – a British Crown Colony, an island paradise filled with sunshine and the soft rustle of ocean breeze turning the multi-colored leaves of the Joseph Coat bush inside out on extremely breezy days. I looked forward to the pleasure of waking up in this paradisiacal landscape, to the reality of being serenaded by the sounds of cackling hens after their eggs were laid. The cries of street vendors – women bearing baskets of fruits on their heads, calling out to the home-bound customers, unaware of the women passing by. I was always excited and happy to see the man in the horse-drawn cart delivering freshly-baked crispy crust bread as my brothers and I rushed out to greet him – the milk man who brought bottles of creamy pasteurized milk and left them on the steps to the house. This was what it meant to grow up in the luxurious beauty of a tropical paradise.

I am sure that in most cases everyone has something good to say about their mom. My mother was a woman of sterling character: proper, self-respecting and dignified. She imparted her wisdom and knowledge of life to all her off-springs which proved a helpful guide in having them stay on the straight and narrow path of life. She was fond of reminding us – her children that she gave all of us very good home training – the essentials of knowing how to interact with others by being respectful and polite. Fortunately for her, she had the support of her mother, our grandmother, in the unpaid task of rearing children. They made an extraordinary pair together with a helper, a woman by the name of Verlin, who in conjunction with my mother and grandmother dedicated their time to rearing my siblings and me.

My Mom was an excellent example of what every good mother should be – stern, but loving – kind, but disciplinary – a woman concerned about the welfare of her children. She saw to it that we would receive a good education in order to lead successful lives. I can't imagine how our parents coped with the difficult task of dealing with the egos and personalities of seven different children while still managing to maintain their equilibrium. My mom taught us how to be kind, considerate and helpful to others. She was that kind of woman and so much more and we loved her for it.

She often took us to garden parties at Winchester Park in downtown Kingston. I was particularly fond of riding on the Ferris wheel and the Merry-Go Round after which we were treated to delicious ice cream cones filled to the brim with various flavors of ice cream: strawberry, vanilla, rum and raison and ginger-flavors that still linger in the taste bud of my memory. Sometimes I wonder if we really had the pleasure of living such extraordinary and beautiful lives.

We were well-schooled in the religious aspect of life as well. My mother was a woman of faith, wedded to the philosophy of the Methodist Church which served as the foundation upon which her life was based and which guided her in rearing disciplined children. We had to be well behaved. She regularly read her bible and prayers were said at every meal. She was a Wesleyian Methodist and the family had to attend Sunday morning service at the local Methodist church under the divine stewardship of the Reverend Atherton Didier. The beautiful hymns of the Methodist Faith would resonate throughout the cavernous halls of Lyndhurst church and was more pronounced when the organist rocked back and forth and blasted the pipe organ with music that still lingers with me to this day. Sunday school was taught by the minister's son, David Didier. Our parents made it mandatory for us to attend – another aspect of learning to grow spiritually in life.

My mother was fond of baking, but my grandmother excelled in the art of cooking. She was an excellent chef of the highest order. Every day we were treated to the most delicious meals one could ever hope to partake of in this life. Mom was fond of making soursop ice cream which she made in an ice cream bucket filled with coarse salt and ice. My brothers and I would then take turns at turning the handle as the ice cream churned inside the bucket. The result always turned out to be the most flavorful, mouth-watering ice cream anyone could ever hope to taste. Mother also made a signature dish that we loved – a chocolate mousse that shivered like the jolt of an earthquake when it hit the flavor buds of one's mouth.

Her spirit of generosity and concern for the happiness of her children knew no boundaries. When Christmas time rolled around, she would make sure that all of us – her children, would write importuning letters to Santa Claus, the bearded one in the red suit, for whatever Christmas presents our hearts desired. It was truly extraordinary to believe in this legendary man wearing a red suit and silvery, white beard that magically appeared at Christmas time dolling out gifts to kids all over the world. After writing my letter to Santa, Mom instructed me to hang my stocking at the end of my bed. She said Santa would come down the chimney on Christmas Eve to fill my stocking with presents, even though our house did not have a chimney, an architectural feature not needed in a tropical climate, unless one lived in the higher elevation of the Blue Mountains where the British soldiers lived in their barracks in New Castle, in the cooler climate they were accustomed to.

I was always filled with joy after writing to Santa and receiving my gifts. I truly believed in him and decided I had to meet him – this benevolent man from the North Pole who would leave his frigid home in the north to come all the way to Jamaica to deliver Christmas gifts for deserving kids. Wow! When the following Christmas rolled around, I made my wish list and gave it to my mother. On Christmas Eve I hung my stocking at the end of the bed, but was too excited to go to go to sleep, too preoccupied with meeting Santa. I tossed and turned in bed that night thinking what I would say to him and how much I would thank him for the presents he brought last year. However, I never got that chance. About an hour after I went to bed, I saw my mother enter my bedroom, hoping that I had already fallen asleep. When she saw that was not the case, she gently tip-toed out of the room. I thought it strange, but did not say anything, afraid that it would frighten Santa and that he would not return. Much later, however, my mother's frustration got the better of her. She then returned to the room and glanced at me thinking I was fast asleep. She then walked over to the end of the bed where my stocking hung and started to load it up with presents. Needless to say, she got the greatest jolt of her life when suddenly I turned around and yelled at her. "Don't touch that stocking, Mommy." I said, "If you do, Santa won't put anything in it." From that night, I never believed in that con man in the red suit, again. This just about brought my childhood innocence to a crashing end.

My mother made up for that brazen mistake by buying me a new pair of black shoes and decided to take my siblings and me to the Christmas market in down town Kingston – a ritual most parents and their kids participated in during the festivities of the Holiday Season. The scene at the Christmas Market was one of great joy and merriment. Throngs of people filled the streets everywhere. The entire downtown was festively decorated with Christmas lights and all kinds of

Christmas paraphernalia. There were gaily dressed vendors in Christmas stalls selling different types of toys and goodies to the happy throngs of people – all dressed in their Christmas best, wearing Christmas hats made of crepe paper. I threw a tantrum after seeing a sailor doll that struck my fancy. The more my mom resisted my desire to have the doll, the louder I screamed. The vendor then reprimanded my mom. "If you don't buy that sailor doll for that kid you will break his heart." Mother finally gave in. I took the sailor doll home, and to my mother's surprise, immediately ripped it apart. Needless to say, my mom was furious and asked me why did I destroy the doll after crying for her to buy it for me? I told her I only wanted to see what it was made of. To my disappointment it was not a real person. It was only made of straw.

On Boxing Day, the day after Christmas, Mother once again took the entire family to see the pantomime, Anancy and Pandora at the Ward Theatre – a time honored tradition that brought crowds of people downtown at Christmas time. I could not contain my happiness. The fact that I was only a child, made it seem as if life was one great big festival. I thank my mother for having experienced such blissful moments. When we returned home, later that evening she treated us to delicious Christmas cakes she had baked the day before and which she served with a drink of Sorrel, the distinctively flavorful drink that was served at Christmas time. How could I not think that she was the best mother in the world!

I loved my mom and miss her dearly, but have to accept the finality of her ephemeral existence. What grater tribute could I pay to her than to honor the legacy of her life – a life that touched so many others in such a positive and inspiring way? I live to honor her memory – a kinder more empathetic person did not exist. I miss her dearly. I really do, even as a little boy, I felt the need to protect her. I know she was strong, but fragile too. I once saw her cry, but there was nothing I could do. She was as beautiful as sunrise and sunset combined. I miss her like roses would the morning dew. Rest in Peace dear Mom! You will always remain in my remembrance. I will never stop loving you!

The Deathly Wave

Artwork by H. Lloyd Weston

Part 1

The gray shingle-roofed house captured a commanding view on a wind-swept hill overlooking the dreamy blue-green waters of Montego Bay. The house was originally built in the 1950s by a wealthy English industrialist as a wedding gift for his Jamaican-born wife, one Marjorie Murdock, nee Middleton, a woman of beauty, background, and standing in the local community. The house was a showcase in which the couple entertained lavishly. The fact they both were members in good standing at the locally exclusive Montego Bay Racket Club, a privileged entity for wealthy Jamaicans and foreigners alike. It has been over a decade since the house was last inhabited, since then it has become a local pariah – a deserted residence harboring shadows and an eerie emptiness. A thick growth of hedges provides a fence of near privacy, although not effective enough to exclude the prying eyes of the curious, particularly the local town's people, the gossip mongers, and those eager for a chance to get a closer look at the Georgian Stone Manor, where Marjorie Murdock died. Because of the story of a haunting, the house has inadvertently become a local attraction by default.

A massive black wrought-iron gate remains chained and padlocked like a prisoner. Its formidable presence guarding the entrance to the property. A black and white for sale sign hangs from a flowering Poinciana tree, towering above the uncut grass of the front lawn, and a "No Trespassing" sign remains prominently posted – a visual reminder to those tempted to breach the prerogative of its privacy. An aura of mystery has surrounded the house ever since the death of its prominent residents, Harold and Marjorie Murdock, owners of the huge stone house. Mystery enveloped the house, encircling it like the thick green growth of spreading ivy, clinging tenaciously to the hidden surface of the stone wall facade.

Many rumors have erupted concerning the circumstances surrounding the untimely passing of Harold and Marjorie Murdock. The gossip mongers claim that the house became haunted, possessed, as it were, by some strange, unnatural force. As a result, the entity has remained unoccupied, an empty shell of its former self – a lonely edifice bereft of any potential buyers – a pariah, isolated in the ghoulish splendor of its limited appeal. How the rumor started, no one knows, but because of it, the house became a magnet for the curious – those suckered in by the compelling tale of its mystery – the unknown circumstances regarding the death of Marjorie Murdock, mistress of the huge stone house. Some even claimed the macabre circumstances could have come straight out of a Gothic horror story. It seemed anything having to do with the supernatural always had the power to titillate the imagination of the superstitious, especially those so predisposed. That's how it was on an island steeped in the folklore of such unorthodox beliefs – an island famous for Obeah, the Jamaican version of the much-feared Haitian Voodoo. The rumor mills, however, continued churning. The gossip mongers claimed that Marjorie Murdock met her fate at the hands of some strange, unnatural force. Some even claimed it was Obeah. However, no one was brave enough to offer proof. The rumor mills, however, continued unabated, spreading gossip like the sure-footed advance of a vicious beast, always trotting from mouth to mouth.

The convoluted story started the day after Harold Murdock lost his life in a fiery boating accident at the locally famous Doctors Cave Beach in Montego Bay, a favorite haunt for both tourists and locals alike. The unexpected tragedy tormented his widow to the point where she found it difficult to function, subsequently driving her into self-imposed exile, a virtual prisoner, hiding within the walls of her own great house. As a result, she became a woman afflicted by loss – the loss of companionship due to her husband's demise, the loss of her peace of mind as a result of it, and the loss of her status as the wife of the all-powerful, Harold Murdock. In the irrationality of her grief, she blamed herself for the circumstances leading up to her husband's untimely demise, never for a moment stopping to think that something more sinister could have been at work – something as pernicious as Obeah. That's how it was on an island known for its grudges, slights, and revenge – a place where it seemed someone was always out to fix someone else's ass. That's just the way it was!

Prior to the incident, there was even talk that Harold Murdock had become too big for his britches – too arrogant in his dealings with the local underlings – the menial laborers who depended upon him to make a living – some barely able to eke out enough to provide for their families on the meager wages he paid to them. It was generally believed that if someone from a working class background had the misfortune of being rubbed the wrong way or even suspected that they were being treated unfairly, especially by a white foreigner against any local underling that would be enough of a spark to ignite the fire of outrage and revenge. Although this in and of itself could be nothing more than mere speculation, something most assuredly seemed strangely amiss.

In the irrationality of her grief, Marjorie Murdock faulted herself for the circumstances leading up to her husband's demise. She felt somehow, she and she alone was responsible for the tragedy, the fact that it was she who insisted upon going to the beach that day, one of those glorious, sun-filled tropical days that seeped under her skin, driving her from the comfort of her manor house for the leisurely life of the white sand beach. The more she reflected upon the incident, the more destabilized her psyche became. It darkened her mind like an ominous cloud, and she dreaded the day when it would return to haunt her, like shadows that lingered after a terrifying nightmare. Unfortunately for her, that fateful day had finally arrived. It was Monday, June 23rd, 1960 – the anniversary of her husband's tragic death – five years ago to the date – a day which evoked the saddest memories for her. The day started out gray and gloomy – an overcast day, one punctuated by frightening flashes of lightening, voluminous blasts of thunder, then a steady, heavy downpour of rain unlike any other seen in Montego Bay's recent history.

Marjorie Murdock remained holed up in her huge stone house, observing the puddles of water forming beneath her bedroom window. Suddenly, her mind flashed back to the day of the tragedy at the beach – the day her husband perished in that awful boating accident. "If only death had claimed me," she sobbed. "If only it had reversed itself and had taken me instead of my beloved husband, Harold." She reflected on the incident leading up to that ill-fated day, remembering the strategy she surreptitiously employed in an effort to persuade her husband to accompany her to the beach that day. She remembered his poignant protestations, the fact that he did not want to leave the house to go and sit idly on the beach that day. She remembered him pleading that he would rather stay at home and complete a work project, rather than spend time lolling on a white sand beach. But Harold lacked the will and the stamina to resist the persuasive charm of his beautiful wife. “Okay, honey!” he replied. “If you insist. I will go, but I will only stay for a while.”

Marjorie Murdock remembered how she hurriedly got dressed, grabbed her strawberry-colored straw hat with matching beach bag, a couple of over-sized beach towels, donned her Dior sunglasses, then sped off with her husband in their white Jaguar convertible for Doctors Cave Beach – a short distance from their secluded residence in the hills of Montego Bay. They paid the admission fee and entered the protected compound, and were immediately caught up in the frivolity of the festive beach scene – dazzling blue skies, turquoise water, a cool ocean breeze, and the blinding glare of the white sand beach. Bathing beauties in form-fitting, one-piece bathing suits strutted their stuff along the shore, acting as if the beach belonged to them and them alone. There were also children sailing multi-colored beach balls high over each other’s heads while frolicking in the waves breaking by the shore. The beach was resplendent with white sailing boats racing in the distance around the scenic bay. One could not help but feel privileged in such a festive environment.

Marjorie Murdock remembered how she daintily waltzed across the heated surface of the sand wearing a fetching one-piece, a white bathing suit which contrasted perfectly with the silken glow of her sandalwood skin. Harold protectively walked by her side, wearing his usual knee-length bathing shorts. The beach beauty and her white English husband walked the length of the beach, searching for a perfect spot to open their over-sized beach towel and stretch out on the warmth of the white sand. They finally found a place under a large, multi-colored aluminum umbrella sprouting in the sand like a mushroom at the far end of the beach.

Marjorie Murdock spread the oversized towel and they both settled down, comforted by the cooling breeze and the soothing sound of the overlapping waves. After a few minutes of lying on the sand, Marjorie Murdock suddenly decided to get up and fetch some refreshments for her and her husband. He watched as she blew a kiss toward him before walking away.

Harold also got up and decided to go for a swim, but before he could plunge into the water, he suddenly ran into an old boating buddy of his, one John Beachley, a tall, muscular man with a heavy growth of beard, and a perpetual tan. "Hey, Harold!" John Beachley called out to his friend. "What a surprise running into you at the beach today!"

"Hi John," said Harold, greeting his old boating mate. "I thought you would be off the island on that business trip you were talking about."

"Unfortunately, Harold." John intoned. "Something came up and it had to be postponed."

"By the way, where is your wife, Marjorie?" John enquired.

"She went to get some refreshments and should be back any time soon. As a matter of fact, there she is coming toward us now."

"Hi Marge!" John Beachley smiled, greeting the belle of the beach.

"Hi John!" Marjorie said, handing a Red Stripe beer to the bearded man. "Fine weather! Isn't it?"

"Splendid!" Marjorie replied.

“Hey Harold!” John continued. “How would you and Marge like to take a spin around the bay in the lovely new boat I recently bought? It’s that blue boat docked by the marina at the far end of the beach.”

“We would love to!” Harold replied.

“Not me!” Marge chimed in. “Why not honey?” Harold said annoyingly.

“I just don’t feel like it,” Marjorie said firmly. “I would rather stay on the beach and work on my tan.” Harold, however, was visibly upset because of his wife’s refusal to accompany them and angrily shot back at her. “Don’t tell me you dragged me to the beach today, but won’t accept John’s invitation for a lovely boat ride around the bay.”

“No, honey, no!” Marge twisted her mouth in a negative sort of way. “I just don’t feel like it.” The chord in Harold’s neck stiffened.

“Okay, honey, if you insist, but think of the fun you are going to miss.”

Part II

Marjorie Murdock watched from the shore as the two men strolled away. John knew that Harold was upset because of Marjorie’s refusal to accompany them but said nothing further about the incident. Marjorie’s feminine intuition told her she was right in her decision. Not being able to swim, she never felt comfortable venturing out on the water. A few minutes later, however, she had become conflicted and started to change her mind. “Harold!” she shouted as the two men strolled away. “Harold!” she called out, but her voice trailed off – drowned out by the sound of the waves and the rumbling noise of the festive beach scene. She watched as the blue boat sped away; the words "Day Dream" emblazoned prominently across the side of the boat.

John Beachley raced the boat as fast as it would go. Round the bay went the speeding blue boat, its outboard motor humming joyously against the clear blue waves. Marge watched from the beach as the boat sliced the waves, transforming the surface of the water into a white spectacle of agitated form with a clear path trailing behind. "What excitement! What a thrill! What fun!" Harold remarked as the men enjoyed the novelty of the ride. "Wish Marge was here to share in the fun."

"Don't worry, Harold," John said. "You know how some women are; they just don't seem to be as adventurous as men." John took a swig of his Red Stripe beer.

"Where did you find this incredible beauty, John?" Harold enquired, as he admired the sleekness of the over-varnished deck.

"Oh, some guy in Miami had it for a while then got divorced, and had to sell it to help pay the alimony. You know the high cost of leaving!"

"Got the drift," Harold replied.

As the men enjoyed the novelty of the ride, the glistening blue-green water of Montego Bay suddenly came to life. The water churned with an amplitude of sailing boats. Some were pleasure crafts taking tourists sight-seeing around the bay. Others were filled with locals trying to escape the hellish heat of the tropical sun. John Beachley raced the boat as fast as it would go, steering skillfully through the overcrowded lanes. But Harold suddenly felt a jolt of concern. “Slow down, John!” he cautioned his boating mate. “Things seem to be getting a bit crowded around here.”

“Don’t worry, Harold,” John replied. “This happens to be a very reliable, high-performance boat.” John’s only concern was to enjoy the pleasure of the ride; the danger was a remote stranger, the furthest thing from his mind.

“Look out, John!” Harold shouted, pointing to a red pleasure craft speeding dangerously from the opposite direction. The boat was moving so fast, it seemed to have bolted out of the blue. John swerved to avoid hitting the oncoming boat, but Day Dream raced frightfully out of control. It snaked like an uncontrollable seahorse, faster and dangerously faster, until it smashed head-on into the wayward boat and burst into a ball of flames. Marjorie Murdock watched from the shore as the two boats burst into a nightmarish orange ball of flames; she saw the flames, heard the screams, and felt the pain. “O my God!” she screamed in a voice of frozen disbelief. “Oh no! Harold! Oh no!” She then collapsed in a crumpled heap upon the heated surface of the white sand beach.

Part III

As the storm continued to rage outside of Mrs. Murdock’s bedroom window, the widow appeared visibly shaken and distraught by the vivid memories of that ill-fated day. She became traumatized by the memories it evoked. She wanted to pull the draperies and walk away from the window but found it almost impossible to move. It seemed she was transfixed without realizing it – a situation which was concluded in the unconscious arena of spoken dialogue. "Why are you tormenting me?" the widow screamed as if engaged in dialogue with her dead husband. "The accident occurred years ago. Leave me alone! Please leave alone!" The distraught woman suddenly let lose a loud, piercing scream which traveled like a siren throughout every crevice of the house. Hilda, her newly acquired maid, was in the kitchen preparing supper when she was suddenly stung by the sound of the venomous scream. A dish fell from the hand of the corpulent girl, and away she flew through the thick and stifling air to the upstairs bedroom chamber where Mrs. Murdock sat, folded like a cat in a crumpled heap, shaking and sobbing uncontrollably.

"Are you alright, Mrs. Murdock?" Hilda's bosom heaved back and forth as the overweight girl came to a sudden stop. "Me hear' you scream ma'am, an me taut…"

"I am fine!" Mrs. Murdock said, and quickly straightened up herself in order to regain her lost composure, not wanting her maid to see her crying, too embarrassed to reveal her tears.

"You sure me can't 'elp 'you, ma'am?"

"I said I'm fine!" Mrs. Murdock snapped at the girl. "Now leave me alone!" She cut off Hilda without any regards for the poor girl's inquiry, a sound believer in the superiority of her upper class background, even under the strain of her suffering. Hilda, although visually upset by the widow's blatant rebuff, decided to ignore the situation and file away the brusque remark. She reflected on the various occasions in which she had observed the widow standing in front of her husband's portrait, staring at the image to the point of tears.

This woman look a bit disturbed, the superstitious girl reflected. *Me 'ope nobody put Obeah 'pon 'er.*

Hilda remembered the compelling tales of Harold Murdock's raw arrogance and his sneering attitude in dealing with his local underlings, the menial workers who depended upon him for their survival. "Poor Mrs. Murdock," Hilda lamented pitifully. "This is no place for anyone to sit on their high horse and kick the little ones below." She wiped the perspiration from her forehead then continued, "There are too many people walking around with slights and grudges, willing to do whatever it takes to bring the high and the mighty down, down from their exalted perch to the level of the little man – the ones they so readily ill-treat."

"Come, ma'am," she said to Mrs. Murdock. "You supper ready, the storm soon over!" Mrs. Murdock glanced up at Hilda with a haggard-looking expression on her face as if to say, "Yes, but for me it's just beginning."

Part IV

The two women drifted toward the dining room, filled with the aroma of Blue Mountain Coffee and the inviting smell of freshly baked pastry. Marjorie Murdock took a seat at the mahogany dining table, opposite a wall where an oil painting of her late husband hung. She bit into the pastry that Hilda had prepared and felt the little white flakes clinging to the corner of her tensed-up mouth. She glanced up at Harold's portrait and immediately felt the weight of accusing eyes staring back at her. The intensity of the stare penetrated her soul to the point where she could no longer continue to eat. The pastry felt like a lump in her throat. Marjorie Murdock took a sip of coffee to force it down. She then pushed aside the Ainsley tea cup in front of her on the dining table and made a mad dash for her upstairs bedroom chamber. Her long black dress swept the wooden floor.

Hilda cleaned up after serving supper, said goodbye to her employee, then quickly vanished from the house. Marjorie Murdock now found herself alone – a virtual prisoner trapped within the walls of the huge stone house. The storm outside had finally subsided, bringing a modicum of relief to the distraught woman. Marjorie Murdock kicked her shoes off, climbed into her bed, and decided to take a nap. She flung herself across the sturdiness of the four-poster bed, hoping to drift off in the reassuring comfort of sleep. She was about to surrender when suddenly she felt the grip of a sharp claw tightening around the flesh of her tender throat. Mrs. Murdock jumped up and screamed out loudly. She turned on the bedroom light only to find her gray Persian cat meowing menacingly around the room. The startled woman swore at the little beast but knew the only way to placate it was to give it something to eat. She put on her bed room slippers and her house robe and headed downstairs toward the kitchen. *"Meow, meow!"* The petulant Persian followed closely behind.

Mrs. Murdock entered the kitchen where it seemed everything was deliberately painted white – the cupboards, the walls, the ceiling and the floor – a kind of blinding haze suffocated the eyes. She opened a can of Purina Gourmet

Cat Food and left it in a clean white dish on the kitchen floor. The cat immediately pounced on the delicious morsels of food. The widow once again headed back upstairs, but instead of going back to sleep, she decided to take a bath, hoping the warm water would soothe her nerves after all the traumas of this day. Although the rain had ceased, an electric storm still raged in the sky. Marjorie Murdock watched fearfully as flares of lightening lit up the sky, branching out into myriad crazy patterns, casting a melancholy mauve-green glow throughout every room of the house.

She entered the bathroom and disrobed then turned on the faucet above the large, white porcelain tub. The gushing sound of the water shattered the quietude of the house and helped to soothe her battered nerves. She sprinkled a few drops of Parisian bath oil into the swirling vortex, and gently slithered into the tub, crushing the mass of bubbles under the weight of her bony body. The warm water felt good against her sandalwood skin. She stretched out in the tub, which made her feel more relaxed. Suddenly, however, she felt a strange feeling of uneasiness. What it was, she did not know, but the feeling registered prominently in her consciousness. The mood in the house suddenly became one of eeriness. Shortly thereafter, Marjorie Murdock thought she heard what sounded like an object falling somewhere in the house. The noise caused her to panic. Memories of her dead husband then suddenly crept into her mind, and she imagined she saw a deathly wave coming at her across the surface of the water, filling up the tub. She felt restrained as the water locked her hopelessly in its heavy liquid arms. She gasped, and a few bubbles slipped down her throat.

The wind outside had picked up again. The back door to the kitchen, which Hilda had carelessly left opened, slammed with an awful, deafening noise. The sound traveled through the house, all the way up to the room where Mrs. Murdock was taking her bath.

The widow heard the sound and worried that it might be an intruder. She suddenly feared for her life. "Hilda, is that you?" she enquired apprehensively, forgetting the fact that her maid had already left for the day.

"Hilda, are you there?" No one answered. A feeling of fear suddenly gripped the woman, and her complexion quickly changed to a sickly-looking pallor. Her heart raced as she felt hopelessly trapped within the confines of the white porcelain tub. She swore she heard what sounded like an indistinct clip…clop, slowly ascending the recently polished stairs leading to the upstairs bathroom. It was a sound that caused her heart to race frightfully out of control.

"Who is there?" she demanded. A blast of thunder answered. "I said who is there?" no one answered. Marjorie Murdock listened more intently as the sound crept closer toward the bathroom. She peered through the half-opened door and saw a shadow pressed against the wall at the entrance. "Help!" cried the frightened woman, completely vulnerable in her naked state. "Someone help me, please!" But the house was too isolated for anyone to hear. She fell while trying to escape from the bathtub, striking her head against the rigidity of the cold marble floor. Blood gushed everywhere after she sustained a major gash to the back of her head as she lay motionless and unconscious on the cold marble floor.

Water from the running faucet spilled over the edge of the tub. It gathered speed as it rushed past the petulant Persian cat standing innocently at the entrance to the bathroom door. It continued down the stairs through the dining room, past Harold Murdock's portrait, which now seemed to harbor a bizarre look of contentment on the face of the well painted portrait. It raced in liquid freedom through the living room, down the steps leading to the outside, where it finally merged with puddles that had already accumulated from the storm.

Hilda returned the following morning and immediately sensed that there was something terribly wrong after seeing water running under the kitchen door of the house. She opened the door, where she saw the water running down the stairs leading to Mrs. Murdock's upstairs bedroom chamber. The girl immediately dashed upstairs to see what was wrong. "Mrs. Murdock, Mrs. Murdock," she called in a heightened state of panic. But there was no reply. "Mrs. Murdock," she once again shouted, but still there was no answer. She followed the source of the water to the bathroom and screamed when she saw her mistress, sprawled naked and lifeless in a pool of blood stretched out on the bathroom floor, her body covered with a strange series of gashes and black and blue marks.

The superstitious girl freaked out and immediately ran out of the house, screaming loudly at the top of her lungs. "This is Obeah. First, they fixed Mr. Murdock, and now it seems they did the same thing to Mrs. Murdock."

"It's Obeah! It's Obeah!" The rumor she started never died down.

The Green and Yellow Bus

Part I

It was the time of year that residents of the city dreaded. The oppressive summer heat had finally arrived, driving everyone to distraction. The furnace of the tropical sun churned out the heat, creating extremely uncomfortable conditions for both people and buildings alike.

Only those who lived in air-conditioned dwellings or who worked in air-conditioned places of business were spared the inescapable effects of the all-pervasive heat. Weeds along the sidewalks of city streets literally keeled over as if from exhaustion, into a boiling cauldron of hot gravel and melting tar. Women who ventured out had to resort to the use of over-sized parasols in order to ward off the sting of the overhead sun.

Conditions, however, were sometimes relieved by wisps of ocean breeze skimming appreciatively off the face of the ocean. This was the reality of summer in the tropics – the city of Kingston, Jamaica, to be exact. It was as if the entire island had come under a heat invasive spell. "Lawd! It's hot, it's hot," complained the residents of the city. Everyone tried to find some form of relief.

This was also the time of year when beleaguered parents across the city seemed all too happy to ship their kids off to the country to spend the mid-summer holidays with obliging relatives. This is my story – that of a seven-year-old boy, bound for his first adventure in the country – an opportunity to spend the holidays with relatives in the parish of St. Thomas to be exact. In my undiluted state of joy, never did I feel any discomfort from the heat, which baked the city of Kingston, as if it were a lobster, to a mellow shade of tropical red.

The night prior to my departure was spent in the last-minute excitement of packing for my trip. Many adventurous thoughts raced through my head. I wondered what it would be like to be away from home for the first time or to wake up in the strangeness of a new environment. In the interim, I was forced to endure the well-targeted sounds of my mother's advice. "Don't forget to take your pajamas, Trevor. Where is your tooth brush? Put that in the side compartment of your suitcase, and for God's sake, make sure to behave yourself; if not, your aunt Mavis won't invite you back." I knew Mother was talking, yet nothing seemed to register. The only comparison I could make to the dreary drone of her monotonous voice was that of the old blue fan buzzing quietly away in one corner of the room, comforting though in an irritating sort of way. "And finally," she continued. "Don't forget your manners." I felt I was about to scream. I glanced up at Mother, just in time to see a sheepish grin rippling across her face. She leaned forward and gently kissed me goodnight.

I awoke the following day full of anticipation, rearing to go. Mother had already gotten up. Dad, however, was still asleep after getting home late from work last night.

"Good morning, Trevor."

"Good morning, Mom."

"Did you sleep well last night?"

"Yes, Mother, dear."

"Go take your shower," she commanded. I rushed to the bathroom to get ready as quickly as I could. Dad had finally gotten up and was leafing through the morning papers.

"Breakfast ready!" Mom shouted. The delicious smell of banana pancakes and Blue Mountain coffee sent a tempting aroma wafting through the house. The aromatic smell forced me to the dining table, where I immediately dug into the delicious array of food, which included fresh fruits, Johnny Cakes, and ackee and salt fish, which I washed down with a cup of hot Bonnie Breakfast Cocoa. Dad also followed suit, partaking in the delicious offering, after which he rushed to the shower, knowing we had to leave the house no later than 10:30 a.m.

"Are you ready, Trevor?" Mom's voice registered as if she were happy to be getting me out of the way. She completed her breakfast and then also rushed to the shower to get ready. She wore one of her favorite outfits, a pale, pink-striped dress, the vertical stripes of which were aligned to match the respectable concept she had of herself. I spied on her in the hallway mirror as she fussed with her hair before putting on her makeup. She applied rouge to her cheeks and painted her lips a soft shade of pink, which matched the dress she was wearing.

My suitcase was already packed and waiting at the front door. Mom checked herself in the hallway mirror one last time, feeling confident like any other feminine woman, happy to put her best face forward before venturing out into the world. “Are you ready, Rob?” she called out to Dad.

“Let’s go, kiddo!” My father shouted out to me. He grabbed my brown suit case and threw it in the back seat of the car, which was already waiting in the driveway. Mom got in and sat in the front seat next to him. I slithered into the back seat looking spiffy in my new short pants, my white knit shirt, and my new pair of brown shoes. Dad started the car, and away we went, heading for the bus depot located at South Parade in downtown Kingston.

We drove off into the haze of the mid-morning heat, a mild ball of dust ballooning behind. After half an hour’s drive, we arrived at our destination in the hustle and bustle of downtown Kingston, amidst the annoying blast of car horns and the musical cries of the peanut vendors. Gaily dressed street vendors paraded up and down the public square offering their wares to anyone who cared to buy. “Get ’you peanuts, soft drinks, cheese crunch, cigarettes,” each vendor employing a louder tone in order to attract the rushing throngs of people. We alighted from the car after Dad found a parking space, and were immediately caught up in the carnival-like atmosphere of downtown Kingston. We were about to cross the street when a brazen street vendor rushed up to my mother, dangling a sundry of hand-made goods in front of Mom’s face, importuning her, in a desperate attempt to gain her patronage. “Anything for the nice lady today?” the vendor accosted my Mom. Mother, obviously displeased at the vendor’s aggressiveness, held her head high and walked straight ahead as if the woman had not spoken at all. She was that type of person, proper, self-respecting and dignified.

After crossing the street, we encountered a stiff ocean breeze that sneaked in from the harbor at Victoria Pier, sending bits of paper like birds through the air. Mom held down her dress. Dad clutched his white straw hat firmly in his right hand, and I held onto my brown, beat-up suitcase which was in no danger of going anywhere without me. We headed straight for the bus depot in South Parade where I immediately saw the bus of my destination, waiting, almost as if exclusively for me, the words ST. THOMAS spelled out in bold black letters across the prow of its green and yellow face. I was instantly smitten. I had never seen a country bus before and did not know what to expect. Something about the way it looked filled me with joy. The two circular head lights placed on either side of the facade made it seem as if they were a pair of eyes protruding above the slats of the chrome grill, that appeared like an open mouth, and gave the facade of the bus the appearance of a real human-looking face. This made it seem as if the bus were smiling at me. In return, I smiled back with delight.

Dad entered the bus and purchased my tickets then asked the conductor to make sure to look out for me. I hugged my parents a tight goodbye. Dad was never one to show much emotion. However, his love revealed itself in a quiet but effective sort of way. Mom reached out and gently whispered in my ears. “Have a good time, Trevor!” She hugged and kissed me one last time before walking away. “Don’t forget to behave yourself,” her voice followed me into the bus.

Part II

I felt a tinge of sadness at the thought of leaving my parents, but with the initial revving of the bus engine, I quickly got over that tugging feeling. Entering a country bus was a new experience for me. The conductor placed me in a seat on the right side of the bus, close to the driver, so that I could observe him and execute my childhood fantasy of driving, via his expertise. The ceiling of the bus was painted a glossy shade of green, into which I enjoyed looking to see my muted reflection. The seats were made of dark brown leather, which made an embarrassing squishy, sound whenever any of the passengers moved or shifted in their seats. The bus was filled to capacity with school children going on holiday and market women returning to their homes in the country, some with the unsold produce they carried in intricately woven baskets covered by yards of protective canvas, tied to the roof of thebus.

The conductor cross-checked the aisle and the overhead racks to make sure everything was properly secured into place. the driver then shouted out "All aboard!!" He dragged out the words before starting the bus. My heart raced with excitement. The bus edged out slowly. It made a sharp, jerky noise that sounded like parts that were not connected properly were finally falling into place. We started to move when suddenly a slight commotion erupted. A market woman whose daughter had skipped off the bus to get some snacks was now frantically knocking at the door trying to regain entrance. Realizing the situation, the market woman screamed out to the driver at the top of her lungs.

"You can't leave me 'dauter, driver! A beg you open 'de door a let 'er in." The little girl, looking like the devil's daughter, jumped up into the bus and sat beside her mother.

The driver carefully pulled out from the bus depot in South Parade, the main square plunked down into the heart of down town Kingston – the adventure of a lifetime was about to begin. Flags fluttered everywhere as we drove past department stores and bazaars owned by the merchant class of the city – Bata, Bardowells, Kinkhead, Issas and Nathans, – all filled with shoppers rushing into the air-conditioned buildings trying to escape the blistering heat of the tropical sun. The bus gathered speed as we glided past sidewalk vendors, some almost invisible behind huge mounds of vegetables and fruits brought into the city from the rural parishes. The bus tilted to the right as we drove past Victoria Park, this gave us a privileged view of the well-positioned statue of British Queen Victoria – a big, imposing bulk of pigeon-stained white marble, reigning over the hungry birds, pecking at her feet. "That's Ward Theatre!" shouted a little boy as we drove past the famous Kingston landmark, where many pantomimes drew crowds of people during the busy Christmas Holiday Season. The driver made a sharp right, past Coke Memorial Church, the mother church for all members of the Methodist Faith. We then drove directly into Windward road, the main artery leading out of the sweating claws of the city. We gathered speed as the driver coasted along. He revved the engine to my delight, bullying the smaller cars on the roads with loud blasts from his happy-go-lucky horn, "Brahn-Brahn".

"We really moving now!" exclaimed a cigar-smoking market woman. I had never seen a woman smoke a cigar before. She bit the bitter end of the tobacco and sent a drunken puff of smoke staggering through the air. “Yes, driver! We can really hear you now.” The old girl twisted her jellied mouth.

We coasted along Rockford Road, the scenic route which hugged the shoreline of the city and gave us an advantageous view of the blue Caribbean Sea. The passengers now appeared more relaxed as everyone started to enjoy the scenic view and the pampered feeling of the cool ocean breeze. Suddenly, however, the bus started slowing down. It went slower and slower until it came to a complete halt. Some of the passengers chatted excitedly among themselves while trying to figure out the reason for the delay. It wasn’t long, however, before the reason became quite obvious to me. I stared through the bus window and was immediately confronted by the bright red seams of a policeman’s uniform. The police dismounted from his motorbike then stepped briskly toward the entrance of the bus. The driver opened the door and let him in. “This is a routine traffic stop,” the officer announced in a serious gravel-toned voice, one that matched the authority of his looks. The police surveyed the bus with his deeply set eyes, as he counted each passenger while dutifully working the aisle.

“I have to make sure you’re not overcrowded,” he said to the driver. I felt a feeling of relief that no one was being arrested.

Apparently, the speeding bus, together with the baskets of the produce of the market women tied to the roof, may have drawn unnecessary attention to us.

“And another thing,” the police turned toward the driver. “Watch your speed, too many accidents occur on this stretch of the road. This is a warning.”

“Thank you, sir!” the bus driver replied. The officer stepped briskly away from the bus, mounted his blue motorbike and then disappeared into a cloud of dust.

Part III

Our driver cautiously pulled out once more, partly cognizant of the warning by the police; however, it was not long before he started speeding again. The scenery gradually changed as we drove through the rural communities, making it clear, we now were out of the sweating claws of the city. The bus moaned as we ascended into the higher elevations. The passengers appeared totally mellow and relaxed, some of them even drifted off to sleep. The sleepy atmosphere aboard the bus became contagious, and it was not long before my head had also started to suffer the rising and falling motion of oncoming sleep. But it seemed as soon as I had drifted off, I awoke again, just as quickly, completely disoriented by the sound of screeching brakes and a sharp forward pitching motion. Some of the passengers screamed hysterically. I felt for sure we were involved in a serious accident. I looked through the bus window and could not believe what I had seen. There, directly in front of the bus, was a fragmented line of cattle, leisurely, but very leisurely, crossing the street. I had never seen such a sight before. The bus driver blew his horn threateningly in an attempt to clear the road, but the disoriented cattle kept on coming like an avalanche of brown paper packages, stuffed with straw, jostling each other for position, while on the left-hand side of the road, two wild-eyed farmers dressed in blue overalls cracked their whips over the heads of the confused cattle, commanding the dumb beasts to move faster than they possibly could. *"Biff-biff."* A stiff blow landed against a brown cow's neck. "Moo, moo, but 'wat is 'dis?" exclaimed a market woman. Yet some of the other passengers were too accustomed to the cow-crossing incident to be upset.

It took five minutes for the road to clear, after which we once again embarked upon our journey. The next few miles evaporated uneventfully. Finally, we were able to relax and enjoy the changing scenery of the beautiful countryside. It was fascinating to see the quaint little country houses precariously perched on top of the hills. It made me wonder if those poor-looking little dwellings could ever withstand the ferocity of a hurricane or a tropical storm. We drove past an array of exotic trees and flowering bushes. The sight of the Hibiscus flowers lit up my eyes – their profuse blooms of pink and red petals painting the landscape with a joyful splash of tropical colors. It was a novelty to see people riding donkeys through the streets of the town and to hear the sounds of the loud braying reverberating throughout the surrounding areas. It was also interesting to see the bodies of the riders rocking back and forth with the jerky movement of the animals. One of the kids on the bus pointed to a group of stray goats scrounging contentedly on a hillside overgrown with various types of wild bushes and thick green fever grass.

The driver changed gears as we drove through the mountainous terrain. Suddenly, the conductor shouted out in a sing-song tone of voice. “Port Morant, next stop!”

The announcement filled me with joy, knowing the next stop would be Airy Castle, the town of my destination, as confirmed by the conductor to every child’s question. “Are we there yet?” The driver then started our descent into the plains. He toyed with the bus horn, which echoed musically throughout the vast expanse of the valley. As we approached the plains, the shoreline once again popped into view. Through the thick growth of palm trees swaying delightfully in the breeze along the shore, one could glimpse bits of the sparkling Caribbean Sea, clear blue patches, invitingly mysterious, dancing ceaselessly under the bright glow of the sun.

We coasted along until we came upon the sleepy seaside town of Port Morant, a charming fishing village that represented a pleasant stop along the way. Those passengers, who had reached their destination, gathered their belongings and quickly scampered from the bus. Others stepped outside to stretch their legs or refresh themselves. I decided to remain in my seat to take in the sights of this quaint seaside town. Gaily dressed fish vendors rushed up to the bus windows, dangling their assortment of sad-looking fishes into the air while shouting out loudly at everyone in the square, “Get you Angel fish, King fish, Parrot fish.” The raw odors of their cries clung to the stench of the fetid air.

Part IV

After a break of about ten minutes, we once again embarked upon our journey. The bus emitted a series of sharp backfiring sounds as we pulled out. The driver cruised along unperturbed. We drove carefully along the seashore before starting our ascent into the mountainous terrain for the last stretch of our trip. The conductor finally announced in a jovial tone of voice. “Airy Castle will be our next stop.” Those words sounded like music to my ears. Finally, I would be arriving at what so far seemed like an evasive destination. I immediately envisioned my aunt Mavis waiting to greet me with outstretched arms as she would welcome me to spend the mid-summer holidays with her and her family. But we drove into a sudden heavy downpour of rain. Some of the passengers rushed to close their windows as the bus crawled through the heavy deluge. I had never seen so much rain in such a short period of time, while on the surrounding hills, the sun kept shining just as brightly as before – a puzzling sight indeed! “The devil playing with his wife!” exclaimed a market woman in an effort to explain the conundrum of this tropical enigma – rain on one side of the road, while on the opposite side, the sun kept shining brightly.

The bus slowly made its way out of the heavy deluge. It seemed to strain as we negotiated our way into the higher acclivity of the mountains. It seemed the higher we climbed, the narrower the road became, the fact being that it was carved out of the side of the mountains. It seemed there was hardly any space to navigate. It was terrifying to look down from that vantage point into the ravines below. I shuddered at the thought of what would happen if two buses were to collide around that corner. One passenger pointed to a spot where an accident recently occurred, causing a bus to go over a precipice into the valley below. Our driver proceeded cautiously, as though still cognizant of the recent tragedy.

As we drove along, the scenery changed and became even more glorious, making it unmistakably clear, we now were passing through the heart of the country. The city was nothing but a faint memory. The landscape suddenly came alive with the most breath-taking vistas one could ever hope to see. The broad leaves of the breadfruit trees glistened in the lazy light of the afternoon sun as the pungent smell of cedar trees hung heavily in the air. On the surrounding hills, hundreds of palm trees huddled together in solitary splendor, as if reaching out to touch the waiting earth below. Everywhere one looked, one would encounter an overabundance of tropical flowers or fruited trees: mangoes, bananas, oranges, star apples, sweetsop, soursop, guava, jack fruit, grapefruit, ugly fruit-every different kind of fruits – a welcoming sight indeed!

As we drove through the higher elevations, the bus once again emitted a series of sharp backfiring sounds. *"Pow, Pow."* It sounded as if someone was throwing fire crackers at us. This time the driver seemed concerned. There was another loud blast, then more black smoke. The bus then proceeded to go slower and slower until finally, it came to a complete stop. The passengers stared at each other in state of heightened disbelief. The driver stepped outside, popped the hood of the bus and inspected the engine. He then stepped back inside and tried to start the bus once more, but instead of starting, it seemed all his valiant efforts were rewarded only by a faint choking sound. *"Gru, Gru."*

"The old bus dead!" an old market woman remarked. The driver threw his hands up into the air as if to confirm what everyone had already suspected – the green and yellow bus had finally broken down. There we were, almost at the end of our trip, and yet it seemed as if we would never arrive. We waited, bored and immobile, hoping that help would eventually arrive.

Finally, in the opposite direction, another bus approached; our driver flagged it down and related our obvious predicament. The driver of the other bus immediately promised to summon help. We waited about half an hour before a relief bus arrived. Our driver and the conductor helped to transfer our belongings which included our luggage and the remainder of the produce of the market women tied to the roof of the broken-down bus. We were then instructed to form a que prior to boarding the newly arrived bus.

I, however, felt a certain tinge of sadness at the thought of abandoning my friend, the green and yellow bus, considering all the traumas we endured together during the course of the trip. I reflected on the cow-crossing incident, which although amusing, had the power to bring the bus to a complete stop, to say nothing of the mooing, sounds of the cow-sounds I never heard before while growing up in the city.

I took one last look at the green and yellow bus as it sat abandoned by the road side, dejected and deserted after being my companion all along the way. The memorable and vibrant colors were still shining, but not as brightly as before. The late afternoon sun had suddenly vanished from its face.